PUFFIN BOOKS

FIZZ: I've got a ... ek to make him fall ...lessly in love with me, a w...k in which to SEDUCE him.

Maybe if I put tissues inside my push-up bra they'll look bigger.

JOSH: Mum raised her eyebrows. 'Felicity Foster-Thompson? Do I know her? What does she look like?'

That stumped me for a second. What *did* Fizz look like? My brain sifted possible answers at blinding speed.

'She's weird.'

Jeremy Strong spent most of his childhood getting told off for making things up. Nowadays he still makes things up but gets paid for it instead. Result! He has written well over seventy books now. Nobody complained about his first book for teenagers, so here's his second. Will he stop there? We doubt it. When he's not writing, Jeremy spends much of his time pursuing his favourite hobby, extreme sleeping, at which he has now reached Blue Duvet Level. He also enjoys eating crusty bread. Obviously he's easily pleased.

jeremystrong.co.uk

Teenage books by Jeremy Strong

STUFF

WEIRD

PUFFIN

PUFFIN BOOKS

Published by the Penguin Group
Penguin Books Ltd, 80 Strand, London WC2R 0RL, England
Penguin Group (USA) Inc., 375 Hudson Street, New York, New York 10014, USA
Penguin Group (Canada), 90 Eglinton Avenue East, Suite 700, Toronto,
Ontario, Canada M4P 2Y3 (a division of Pearson Penguin Canada Inc.)
Penguin Ireland, 25 St Stephen's Green, Dublin 2, Ireland (a division of Penguin Books Ltd)
Penguin Group (Australia), 250 Camberwell Road, Camberwell,
Victoria 3124, Australia (a division of Pearson Australia Group Pty Ltd)
Penguin Books India Pvt Ltd, 11 Community Centre, Panchsheel Park,
New Delhi – 110 017, India
Penguin Group (NZ), 67 Apollo Drive, Rosedale, North Shore 0632, New Zealand
(a division of Pearson New Zealand Ltd)
Penguin Books (South Africa) (Pty) Ltd, 24 Sturdee Avenue, Rosebank,
Johannesburg 2196, South Africa

Penguin Books Ltd, Registered Offices: 80 Strand, London WC2R 0RL, England

puffinbooks.com

First published 2008
2

Set in Baskerville MT by Palimpsest Book Production Limited,
Grangemouth, Stirlingshire
Made and printed in England by Clays Ltd, St Ives plc

British Library Cataloguing in Publication Data
A CIP catalogue record for this book is available from the British Library

ISBN: 978–0–141–32202–5

www.greenpenguin.co.uk

Penguin Books is committed to a sustainable future
for our business, our readers and our planet.
The book in your hands is made from paper
certified by the Forest Stewardship Council.

This is for my daughter, Jessica, with much love and thanks for everything you have been and will be, and for all you have done.

I would like to thank my editor, Yvonne Hooker, for her endless patience, sensible judgement and unobtrusive good taste, demonstrated over many years. May you have a long and happy retirement.

Contents

Probably More
Information Than You
Really Want to Know

When I was nine I found two goats mating in my bed. Actually they were more 'on' than 'in'. What they were doing looked rather frantic and scary to me. In fact I thought at first they were having a wrestling match but goats don't do wrestling. Also, they were on *my* bed and were really messing it up. The sheet was untucked, they'd trodden all over the pillow and the duvet was halfway across the floor. They were making weird noises too: grunting, wheezing and squeaking and, like I said, it was a bit scary – so I screamed. (I was nine, remember?)

Mum came hurrying to the bottom of the stairs, but not up them because she was making a Christmas cake and had muddy wellies on. (Yes, I know it's not necessary to wear muddy wellies when you make a Christmas cake, but Mum's always doing six jobs at once. It happened to be what she was wearing and when your hands are covered in tacky flour, pockmarked with raisins and such like, *and* you've got muddy wellies on, you don't want to go clumping up the stairs. Satisfied?)

Instead she stood at the bottom and asked what was wrong.

'There are two goats mating on my bed, Mum.'

Do you know what she replied?

'Which ones?'

Typical. Didn't bother to do anything about it, just wanted to know which ones. She came up and watched. 'Ted and Sylvia,' she humphed. 'I might have known.'

All the animals are named after poets, usually their surnames, but Mum's favourites are given the first names of her preferred poets. Ted and Sylvia are named after Ted Hughes and Sylvia Plath, who famously committed suicide. Not both of them – just Sylvia. I haven't told Sylvia the goat who she was named after in case she feels she should do the same. I wouldn't want to be held responsible and, anyway, how would a goat commit suicide? Take an overdose of straw? Shut itself in a confined room, block up all the ventilation points and die from its own flatulence?

I guess you've probably realized – from the way I said 'All the animals . . .' – that we have more than just goats. We also have a tortoise called Byron, because he's got a leg missing and although Byron wasn't missing a leg he did have a club foot (which isn't a foot you club things with, it's a deformed foot and not

much fun, though possibly better than having a whole leg missing). There's a fox and two hamsters, a gerbil, four guinea pigs, two rabbits, three dogs, five cats, a pigeon and an eagle owl called Auden.

That's today's roll-call. It might be different tomorrow. We had an alligator here once, a donkey, swans, pigs, all sorts. My own favourite was a ferret I called Obi Wan because he would appear and disappear, just like that. Obi Wan was not a poet of course, as far as we (the film-going world) know, but I named him, not Mum, because he was my favourite.

From all this you will have gathered that I live in a zoo. It's not a proper zoo, but it often feels like one. It's actually a small house in an ordinary road in an ordinary town. Mum works at an animal sanctuary – The ARC, which is short for Animal Rescue Centre. There's never enough room at the sanctuary for all the animals they get, so Mum brings her work home with her. We get the overflow.

If you're wondering what Dad does, he doesn't. He escaped about a year before I found the two goats in my bed. 'I want a house with people in it,' he told Mum. 'I work in an office. When I come home I want to find people. I want to sit in an armchair that isn't full of rescued rats and have a bath without having to wrestle an anaconda. I want a bit of normality.'

So he went. Mum says he'd got boring. 'When we married he was quite different, quite an adventurer,'

she told me. 'I met him in the jungle. We were studying puma poo. It was so romantic. We had such fun.'

It wasn't such fun when Dad left. I felt I'd lost my only ally. I'm more like him than Mum. I like things tidy and clean. It really annoys Mum. She shouted at me the other day: 'For God's sake, Josh, you're a teenager! Teenage boys are meant to be untidy. There's something wrong with you.'

'Mum, listen, teenagers are never like what their parents want them to be, are they?'

'Exactly.'

'You want me to be untidy – so I'm tidy. That's not what you want, is it?'

She was stumped. After we'd had this mini row I was up in my room and it occurred to me that maybe Mum was more of a teenager than I was. Anyway, I understood where Dad was coming from or, rather, why he was going to where he was going. We see each other regularly. He only lives two streets away. Sometimes when the animals get too much for me I slip round to his house and we tidy things. We don't say much to each other. Just tidy. You probably think I'm weird or gay or something but I'm just telling you how it is. It's calming – tidying things. It's like ordering your thoughts, stacking books neatly on the shelves of your brain.

It was Dad who got me into astronomy. He has a proper stellar telescope. It's extraordinary what you

can see. You can focus on what looks like an empty patch of night sky, look through the 'scope and there they are, stars, thousands of them. And that was a bit of sky you thought was *empty*. When I look up there it's like I'm seeing escape and the future, a universe full of strange new worlds. I'm already building rockets. OK, they're just models, but one day, who knows?

So, anyway, speaking of strange worlds, back to the goats. Ted and Sylvia were hard at it on my bed, trampling all over where I had to sleep and I asked Mum, why? Why did they have to do that upstairs, on my bed?

'It's genetic,' she explained.

'Really?'

'Thousands of years ago goats lived on mountains where it was safe, and that's where they would mate. The desire to mate somewhere high up has been passed down in their genes. That's how evolution works. If your bedroom was downstairs it wouldn't have happened.'

'So now it's my fault?'

Mum smiled. 'I'm just trying to explain things, Josh.' I wanted to tell her that sometimes I didn't want an explanation. What I wanted was for it not to happen in the first place. Instead I gazed round my room and pointed out that the wardrobe was higher than the bed so why didn't they go up there?

'Now you're being silly,' she answered and went

back downstairs to get on with making the Christmas cake. She didn't bother to take Ted and Sylvia with her. Which is probably just as well. Who wants to eat a Christmas cake that goats have had a hand in making? Or a foot.

Next day I go into school and tell my friend Charlie and he tells everyone else, including the teacher, Miss Bennet, and soon the whole school knows and me and goats are linked for the rest of our lives. It just so happened that two days later the goats were replaced by a hedgehog but by then it was too late. It was the goats that stuck in people's minds. I've been called Goat ever since. If I'd waited two days it might have been Hedgehog, but there you go, that's life in all its glory.

Some kids might have been traumatized for ever by such an event but Mum behaved as if it was just one of those things that happen with animals and, besides, I'd grown up with it. It was my normality. It was only when I went to school and began to bring friends home that I realized not everyone lived in a house where goats mate in your bed and you might find a tortoise trying to eat your socks. I lost quite a few friends that way. It took a while before I worked out why.

'That's sad,' said Mum, when I told her. 'I thought children liked animals.'

Yes, children *do* like animals. They just don't like them in their face (or bed), so close up. Did you think I was

exaggerating when I mentioned Dad and the anaconda? It really happened. Imagine that – taking a bath and finding that you're sharing it with a snake from the constrictor family; those are the ones that wrap their bodies round you and squeeze you so hard you can't breathe – which is generally fatal. I don't think anyone would like an animal *that* close. And you spend your life constantly checking everything to make sure there isn't a mouse in the muesli, a red-kneed bird-eating spider beneath your pillow or a wallaby in the wardrobe.

That's probably why I'm so tidy. It's my only defence against the chaos that is the inside of my house. I guess Mum and I are just opposites. We do everything the other way round. She's messy, I'm tidy. And then there are the doors. She has this policy of leaving all doors open, because she carries big loads around and has both hands full and therefore can't open and shut doors. I have this policy of leaving all doors shut because I think it helps prevent unfortunate events like randy goats responding to their evolutionary programming and migrating upstairs to seek the higher ground of my bed for a bit of rumpy-pumpy.

I've just had an interesting thought. Mum says Ted and Sylvia were simply responding to their DNA programming. 'It's genetic.' Those were her words. That was the goats' excuse. Maybe I should try that next time Mr Prendergast asks why I haven't done my science homework.

'It's genetic,' I'll say, and Prenders will look apologetic and back off and say: 'Terribly sorry, didn't realize. Of course. You can't help it.'

But now I have a different kind of problem. We're on work experience next week. I am so excited, not. We're all being sent out into the big wide world so we can find out what life is really like. As if I need to know. I could tell my teachers a thing or two. I bet they don't know what noises goats make when they're you-know-what-ing. I bet they've never pushed a pig in a wheelbarrow (which I had to do once because it had a poorly trotter), or cleaned up behind an incontinent newt.

School has fixed me up with work at Marigolds, the care home, and you know what that means – wrinklies. I'm going to be thrown to the prunes. Not only that, but I shan't be on my own. Felicity Foster-Thompson is going as well. Felicity Foster-Thompson! Why couldn't it be her big sis, Lauren, who looks like a goddess, walks like a goddess, speaks like a goddess and, oh, have you got this – IS a goddess? OK, she's seventeen and maybe you think the age difference is too great but if you saw her you'd trip over your own eyeballs. Unfortunately she doesn't seem to notice me, but she will. I'll think of something.

Sometimes I dream I'm saving her from impending doom. She's drowning in the sea. I plunge through the waves, my strong arms scything the water as I speed towards her, beating off the sharks that swirl around

us. I grab her as she goes under for the fifth time and, with one arm clutched round her chest (I like that bit), I haul her to dry land. Her wet clothes cling to her and I gaze down at her beautiful face and her eyes flutter open and she looks back at me and whispers, 'Oh, Josh, you've saved my life. Is there anything I can do for you?' And I casually drawl in my manly voice, 'Well, actually, yes.'

Unfortunately in real life I can't swim unless my feet are touching the bottom, and Lauren is in a different part of the school so about the only chance I have of seeing her is when she goes home because she meets up with little sis, Felicity, who's an over-excited, dentally challenged, myopic five-year-old. How she ever got into Year Nine I've no idea. Somebody must have made a mistake. Felicity Foster-Thompson and me on work experience, together, in a care home for the elderly. Whoopee. I'm so excited.

It's no good. Been looking in the mirror. Frankenstein's bride. That's who I am. And even he wouldn't want to marry me. God, I look awful, like I've stumbled straight out of a horror film. I can't decide if it's the antique specs or the pauper's brace. I am probably the last girl on the planet without contact lenses – and the specs are two years old. Two years! And then all my friends go and get totally cosmic braces in different colours and I've got National Health Service. I was obviously born under a very bad sign – quite probably the horrendously unlucky thirteenth sign of the Zodiac, The Slug, Bringer Of All The Grunge In Your Life, which represents me perfectly.

I keep telling Mum I need cosmetic surgery (and contact lenses). She just laughs. I don't think she even knows what cosmetic surgery is, because she's perfect. She says. And Dad agrees.

'You're perfect, darling,' Dad keeps telling her. Then he COMPLETELY ruins it by saying to me: 'And you're perfect too, Felicity.'

'With my squiffy eyes and totally antique spectacles that were unearthed in some archaeological bronze-age dig and my brace that catches the light like sharks' teeth catch the, catch the, whatever light you get underwater. And my boobs are too small.'

PARENTAL CHORUS: 'Ha ha ha ha ha!'

I mean, have they never seen *OK* magazine? 'They are,' I insisted.

'They'll grow more,' said Mum. 'In the meantime, try a push-up bra.'

'I am wearing a push-up bra,' I said through gritted teeth. 'I need cosmetic surgery. It doesn't cost much, only a few thousand. I am being mentally damaged by having small boobs.'

'Don't be silly,' said Dad. Such an intelligent comment to make to a fourteen-year-old, don't you think?

'I'm not being silly. This is my life I'm talking about.'

'When you're eighteen,' said Mum. 'You can do what you want then.'

'Sixteen.'

Mum sighed. 'Not negotiable, Felicity. Sixteen is the age of consent, but not the age of responsibility, or even, I might say, maturity.'

'I'd be more mature if I had bigger boobs,' I said pointedly.

'How does that work?' asked Dad. I threw an icy glance at him and he shrugged. 'I was just wondering

about the correlation between maturity and the size of your boobs. I don't think it's been scientifically established.'

I hate it when he gets like that. Thinks he's clever. I'll show him. Maybe not today, because I can't think of an answer, but I will, one day. I shall study all the sciences and get a million A levels and go to all the totally tip-top universities like Cambridge and Harvard and that famous one in Paris, the Sorbet (where I shall also become a top model with my new cosmetic boobs and fall in love with a totally dishy French waiter called Jules who is terribly poor but awfully handsome and who worships me, despite my affair with the French President, which gets splashed all over the pages of *OK* magazine, but Mum and Dad don't even notice because they live in a World of Unawareness), and I shall study and study and become the world's leading expert on every science known to mankind and then, the next time Dad says: 'I don't think it's been scientifically established,' I shall say: 'Oh, but, Father dear, I am afraid your scientific knowledge is woefully out of date. I was researching the odour distribution of earwig pheromones last week and I have discovered that blah blah blah blah.' And he'll be stunned. And I shall sweep from the room, triumphant. Except that by then, after all that studying, I shall probably be about thirty and covered in wrinkles from top to bottom and beyond and I'll

have left home so it will all be TOO LATE. Born under a bad sign, like I said.

Then Mum told me I looked gorgeous and didn't need improving.

'They're like pimples,' I muttered, so Mum started telling horror stories about women who came to her health clinic with massive scars, or boobs that didn't match because they were different sizes or shapes or colours. (Maybe not colours, but definitely sizes.)

'And I've heard about women going on planes and their breasts have exploded,' she added, quite unnecessarily, obviously trying to scare me. Which she did.

I sat down heavily.

'Your mother means that the silicone implants exploded,' Dad corrected. 'It's the pressurized air in the cabin at great heights. Even so, not very nice.'

'I promise I won't go on planes,' I offered. 'I'm only going to school.'

'You won't be at school for ever, darling,' Mum said. 'You'll need to get on a plane sometime.'

'I promise to only take low-flying ones.'

They looked at me sadly. I'm not surprised. Even I knew it was pathetic.

'Come on, Fizz, you're a gorgeous girl and there's nothing wrong with you,' insisted Mum.

'So how come Josh won't look at me?'

PARENTAL CHORUS: 'Josh?'

How could I have been so stupid to let that one out?

I ignored their gaze, but felt my face rapidly turning into a beetroot.

'Josh?' repeated Dad.

'Boy at school,' I muttered.

'Pardon?' asked Dad, leaning forward.

'BOY AT SCHOOL! BOY AT SCHOOL! SATISFIED, ARE YOU, NOW YOU'VE WINKLED THAT OUT OF ME? THE GESTAPO WERE LIKE TEDDY BEARS COMPARED TO YOU!' And I stormed upstairs. And slammed the door.

That's style for you, and funnily enough they didn't pursue me.

And I've still got a face like a, like a . . . probably like an exploded boob. No wonder Josh doesn't pay any attention. Josh, my man of mystery. I know nothing about him. Everyone calls him Goat. Why's that? Mysterious. Cool, that's what. He's really tall and walks with a long, loping stride, like he could walk for ever, to Australia and back probably. I tried to follow him once but couldn't keep up. I was puffed. He's so neat, which is very unusual for a boy. All the others have their shirts hanging out and ties that seem to stick out of their ears. They think it's cool. It isn't. It's crap. They're all noise and action and scruffiness. Josh isn't like them at all. He's quiet and gorgeous.

I had this dream about him once where he was drowning and I had to plunge into the waves and rescue him and I hauled him to the beach. I have actu-

ally done life-saving classes, you know, with pyjamas and bricks, so there. Obviously it wasn't very exciting jumping into a cold pool to rescue a brick but dreaming about saving Josh was. I got him to the beach and I gave him the kiss of life and IT WAS BRILLIANT and I saved him and he came to but we just carried on kissing until I woke up, which was so stupid of me. Anyway, like I said, he's quiet. I've asked him loads of questions and he hardly tells you anything.

'Why does everyone call you Goat?' I asked.

'How do you explain why people do anything?' he answered. That's a bit cryptic, isn't it? What was that supposed to mean?

'Where do you live?' He nodded in one direction, which could mean, basically, anywhere between where we were and the other side of the world.

'Right,' I nodded. 'What does your dad do?'

'Office.'

'My dad works in a laboratory – oh, you know.' I was so nervous I couldn't even speak properly and was making a right fool of myself. 'He puts things under microscopes and pokes them until they do something and then he draws an inference or a conclusion. He says conclusions are usually better than inferences because then you know where you are. I don't know what he's talking about either, I'm just telling you what he says so you know what I have to deal with at home. Bit of a mad scientist, but without the hair. I mean, he

does have hair – some – but not mad scientist hair, you know?'

I was fiddling with my own hair, pushing it about, pulling at it and messing it up. Must have looked as if a giant collection of twigs had fallen on my head from a great height. Josh was staring at me with a strange expression on his face so I hastily began patting it back down again. I think he thought I was actually mad instead of just pretending.

'Right.'

'And my mum's a beauty technician at Karmarama, you know, the posh health club, which means, really, well, really what she does is nails and stuff. And eyebrow tweaking and waxing legs and bikini lines, which is so, so gross, I don't know how she does it, and tanning and so on. And sticks cucumbers on people's heads. And she does private treatment at home because then she can charge twice as much. What does your mum do?'

'Gotta go,' he said, and he did. In a flash. Like I said, man of mystery. Big sis, Lauren, reckons he's weird, but she thinks almost everything is weird except herself and her friends. She says he looks at her in a funny way.

'What sort of way?' I asked.

'Sideways,' she said. 'As if he's not looking, but he is. Weird.'

'Maybe he's got something wrong with his neck.'

'Maybe he's got something wrong with his head, more like.'

So I asked him if there was something wrong with his neck and he looked at me like I was a lunatic and didn't answer. That's why I say he's quiet, like one of those monks that take a vow of silence. I asked him about that too.

'Are you a monk, or something?'

'Yes,' he said.

He's lying. I know he's lying. Obviously he isn't. If he was a monk he wouldn't be at school, would he? And besides, I don't think you're allowed to be a monk when you're fourteen. Unless you're the Daily Llama or whatever that Tibetan bloke is and, anyway, that's a different kind of monk, I think.

'No, you're not,' I laughed and he shrugged. Didn't say a word. Just shrugged.

I can't stop looking at him – but he won't look at ME! Not even sideways – not even when I wore that REALLY low top to the disco – it was Lauren's but I sneaked it when she wasn't there but she's got bigger boobs than me so it was a bit loose. Everyone else was looking. Even the Head. And she's a woman. Anyway, he went and danced with Evie instead. Evie's my best friend. She's been my best friend for three years. However, if she gets off with Josh I shall have to kill her.

So anyway, how am I going to get Josh to look at

me, let alone go out with me? MY BIG OPPORTUNITY is coming up. It's work experience next week and I am being packed off to Marigolds, the old people's care home. Am I looking forward to this new experience? No. Well, yes, too. Yes and No. I am NOT looking forward to having to work with the elderly. Now I know, because we have PSE at school, that there is this thing called political correctness and it's not the olds' fault that they're ancient and past it and wrinkled beyond rescue by any plastering company known to man, but I'm afraid that it can't change my general feeling that I am being packed off to a Death Camp for the Terminally Deranged. I mean, they'll all be doing their special classes, weaving raffia coffins and such. That's not for me. I'm young. I'm fourteen. I need people my own age.

But the good news is that Josh has been sent there too. Result! I've got a week to get him to notice me, a week to make him fall hopelessly in love with me, a week in which to SEDUCE him.

Maybe if I put tissues inside my push-up bra they'll look bigger.

Monday:
Stealth Slippers

What's biggest – hugely massive or massively huge? I felt life itself being sucked out of my body, like what happens when a small planet gets too close to a giant one and is ripped apart by the overwhelming gravitational power of the giant. It wasn't that Matron was fat; she was gargantuan.

'Yes?' she snapped. Very welcoming. Before I could answer she added: 'Oh. You must be the boy from the school.' She spat the words out like nasty pips. 'Where's the girl?'

'I don't know.'

'What do you mean, you don't know? She's supposed to be with you. The school said there'd be the two of you, together. I can only see one, on his own.'

'We are in the same class,' I offered. 'But we were told to make our own way.'

'And I was told there'd be two of you. She's late. Nurse Evans is on a week's leave, which means I have to do her work and mine, and it's only Monday. What's her name?'

'Nurse Evans?' Why ask? She'd just told me.

'Wake up, lad! You're not at school now. You can't sleep all day. The girl. What's her name?'

'Felicity.'

'Is that it?'

'Felicity Foster-Thompson.'

'Oh – Felicity Foster-Thompson,' said the woman, sucking in her cheeks and putting on an oh-aren't-we-so-posh voice. She rolled her eyes.

'I'm Josh,' I said.

'Did I ask?'

I shook my head and gazed down the road. Fizz should have been here by now.

'Call me Matron,' said the woman. 'That is what I am and that is what you call me. Do you understand?'

I wanted to say: Yes, and I'm human and you can treat me like one, but I didn't because she's a giant planet and very scary. She's so massive you could probably make three normal-sized people out of her.

We stood staring down the road, but there was no sign of Fizz. I wondered what she'd be wearing. Hopefully nothing like that outfit she had on at the disco. Unforgettable. She had this minuscule top. The Head couldn't take her eyes off it. I think she thought something might pop out at any moment, and she wasn't the only one either. You could see everything, almost. I couldn't *not* look and I kept thinking any second now

she's going to notice and think I'm perving on her, staring at her chest all the time – look somewhere else, look somewhere else. Shame really, I mean there she is, nice figure, but she's got a mouth full of nuts and bolts, not to mention the specs, which make her look like a cross between a vulture and a very prim secretary. Plus the fact that she speaks fluent gibberish. I've had more intelligent conversations with some of Mum's rescued animals. I went and danced with Evie instead. She's OK.

I'd like to ask Evie out, but she's going out with my friend Charlie and also there's the problem of my chaotic house. I suppose I could always try shrugging my shoulders and telling her it's genetic but I don't think you can have a genetically compromised house. Would Evie realize? She might just nod sympathetically and say: 'Oh dear, that's a shame,' because she's not scientifically minded. When we were dancing I told her I knew all the periodic table and she said, 'Really? I didn't think boys had them.'

Matron was still staring down the road. 'Dreadful,' she muttered. 'Can't even get here on time. I can see she's going to be as much use as a wet blanket.'

I was going to say, '*You could put out a fire with a wet blanket*,' but I didn't. I was in too close an orbit at the time.

'Can't stand here on the doorstep any longer, there's work to be done,' snapped Matron, and she pushed

me inside the house and slammed the door. I heard the lock slide automatically into place. Matron saw me glance back. 'Security. We keep everything locked. You never know what They might do.' Matron emphasized 'They' as if it meant the enemy. 'They're always up to something. There's one rule here, and that's never believe anything They say. They live in their own fantasy world. They'll tell you all sorts of nonsense. Ah, here's the Major.'

Well! I thought Matron was big, but the Major was gigantic. My English teacher, Mrs Taylor, says we should avoid creating stereotypes when we write stories. I remember it well because Charlie shoved his hand up and said, 'But you always wear very pointy boots!' And everybody laughed because everybody knows Mrs Taylor wears pointy boots because she thinks it's sexy and sexy pointy boots are kind of stereotypical in themselves. Mrs Taylor went a bit red and told Charlie not to make personal comments. Charlie said you have to make personal comments when you describe people. Mrs Taylor said, 'That's right, Charlie – in stories. Not in class to your teacher.' He shut up after that and just had a grin on his face for the rest of the lesson.

The thing is, the Major *was* a stereotype. He was probably a stereotype of a stereotype. If you were asked to draw a picture of what you think a major looks like it would look like this one. He had a ginger

moustache like one of those bellowing sergeants you see in films about the army, only his moustache was even bigger, which was probably why he was a major, and he had massive shoulders you could stack chairs on. Not that you'd want to. And then there was the way he talked.

'Major Trubshaw,' he announced, holding out a hand. 'I run the place. Like clockwork.'

'Ow!' I tried to whip my hand back but he was still busily crushing it, fixing his beady eyes on me.

'What? What?'

'You're squeezing my hand,' I winced. He let go and his eyes narrowed.

'You're not a wimp, are you? Think you need some strengthening medicine, eh? What do you say, Matron? Bit of the old strengthening jollop would do this young man the world of good. Can't have the youth of today cringing when you shake their hand. Won't do at all. Now then, relocation duties for you, young man. That'll get those muscles working, what?' I already wanted to send him on front-line duty.

I was propelled down the corridor until we reached a door, which Matron unlocked. It was a storeroom, piled high with towels on one side and on the other, bathroom-type stuff – toilet rolls, tissues, bars of soap, multipacks of shampoo and so on.

'List please, Matron,' barked the Major, and she handed over a piece of paper. 'Your checklist,' he told

me. 'Go to every bathroom and check for missing items. If there's no soap left, come down here, get a bar of soap. Take it to the bathroom. Got it?'

So this was work experience – dishing out bars of soap? I was so excited I almost wet myself. 'I can't wait to get started,' I told the Major. *Ffwissh.* Went right over his head.

'That's the spirit. Jolly good.' He propelled me back into the corridor. As I emerged I thought I saw a vague movement at the far end but when I looked there was nothing there. A ghost? That might perk things up. I headed for the stairs, while the Major and Matron disappeared elsewhere.

Upstairs it was eerily quiet. There were two long corridors, stretching away in opposite directions. I walked down one. Most of the doors had numbers, but some said 'Bathroom', or 'WC'. I began checking my list and time passed, slowly.

I must have been working away for about half an hour when I heard a commotion downstairs and realized that Fizz had arrived, at last. It sounded like she was getting a bit of a bawling out, which wasn't all that surprising. I went to the top of the stairs but I couldn't see anything, only heard raised voices. Then things went quiet. I got back to work. It was not exactly exciting work, but at least it kept me busy. At that point I was startled by a small voice.

'Hello.'

I wheeled round. A prune was standing right behind me.

'I never heard you,' I said. The old woman looked down at her feet and smiled.

'Stealth slippers,' she whispered, putting one finger to her lips to indicate it was a secret. She leaned forward. 'The Americans have a stealth bomber, you know. I have stealth slippers. Don't tell them. If the Americans knew, they'd kidnap me.'

I nodded and looked around frantically for help. She was obviously mad.

'They're top secret, you know. They mustn't fall into the wrong . . . feet.' She stifled a chuckle and her eyes slowly searched mine and then I understood that, no, she probably wasn't mad at all.

'You've met the Camp Commandant and his side-kick?'

'Yes.'

'What did you make of them, young man?'

'My name's Josh,' I told her.

'And I am Mrs Kowalski. You haven't told me what you think.'

'Well, they, um, they're, er . . . big?' I struggled. Mrs Kowalski touched me gently on one arm.

'I shall tell you what I think,' she confided. 'They are keeping us prisoners here. You've seen the locks on the doors and windows? You be careful, Josh. Be careful what you say and do. Now then, what I need to

know is – uh-oh, here come the goons and I shouldn't be out of my room.' She must have seen my puzzled expression. 'Goons. It's what POWs used to call their prison camp guards in the war. My husband told me that. He was in one, you know.' She leaned closer and whispered, 'Whatever happens, don't be surprised.'

'Which war?' I began, but I already knew. The Second World War. Good grief, that was ages ago. I glanced at Mrs Kowalski. Was she really old enough to have been in the Second World War? Had her husband been in a prison camp?

And then the goons arrived – Matron and the Major – and they didn't look happy.

'Mrs Kowalski, you're out of your room.' Matron made it sound like a capital offence.

'Am I?'

I was astonished. The old lady's voice had gone all querulous, like a little lost girl. The Major heaved a sigh.

'Mrs Kowalski, have you been taking your tablets or have you forgotten, again?'

'Oh no, Major, I mean yes, I have, with some water, like you said, with some water and my tablets too, I've taken those. You told me.'

'And have you taken anything else, Mrs Kowalski?' snapped Matron, narrowing her eyes.

Mrs Kowalski shuffled closer to me. 'Have I? I don't think so, Matron. Oh no, only water and tablets. Two

tablets they were, a pink one and a white one, or was it a white one and a blue one?'

As I listened to Mrs Kowalski gabbling I felt something hard press against my back. She was pushing something against my spine, then slipping it inside the back of my trousers. She'd pushed something into my trousers!

'What about a spoon, Mrs Kowalski? A tablespoon from the dinner service. Have you taken a tablespoon?'

'Oh no, Major, not at all. I do have a teaspoon in my room. Would that be of any use?'

The Major ignored the offer. His face wore a tired frown. 'It's the fourth one to go missing in the last few weeks. I thought the first might be an accident, but when four go missing, that's not an accident, that's theft. I don't suppose you know anything about spoons or where they might be, Mrs Kowalski?'

'No, I'm afraid I don't, Major. I took my tablets, just like you said. A pink one and a blue one, but I didn't take a spoon. Do you know, when I was a child I had a special spoon and the handle was a tiny giraffe. His feet held the spoon end and his neck and head were the handle. And I lost it. Such a shame. I don't suppose you know where it is?' Mrs Kowalski blinked at the Major with sad, wet eyes.

The Major groaned with frustration and turned to Matron. 'Take her back to her room, Matron, while I continue this ridiculous hunt.'

Matron bundled Mrs Kowalski away and the Major turned to me. I kept my back to the wall.

'I trust you haven't seen a large tablespoon anywhere?' asked the Major.

'No.'

'If you find any please bring them straight to me. I really can't stand it. There should be a dozen of everything, including tablespoons, and now there are only eight. What would you think if you saw two ranks of soldiers and one was shorter than –' The Major broke off suddenly and shook his head. 'No, you wouldn't understand, youth of today and all that. Hmm!' He grunted and snapped his head up as if he was standing to attention.

'How many bathrooms have you got left to do?' he barked.

'Four.'

'Carry on.' The Major spun on one heel and marched off to the stairs.

I reached behind me and pulled the hard object from my trousers. I knew what it was going to be of course, but I was confused. One part of me was thinking, why on earth would an old woman want to steal a tablespoon? The only answer I could think of was because she's deranged, just like Matron said. On the other hand, Mrs Kowalski had sounded pretty much together when she was talking to me and, besides, why hadn't I owned up and shown the Major the spoon?

Something mysterious and quite possibly dangerous was going on at Marigolds and now I was probably involved in it, whatever it was, up to my neck. Weird.

I have never seen such a huge woman in my life. It was like she'd been pumped up. And her boobs! No wonder mine are so small. This woman had obviously hogged most of the world's boob-filling for her own nefarious purposes. Talk about selfish. She said she was Matron and yelled at me right from the start.

'You're late!'

'Am I?' I looked at my watch, not that I have one, but it's the thought that counts.

'There are two rules here: never be late and don't question me,' thundered Matron. 'I ask the questions and you answer. Got it?'

'Mrs Singh, our maths teacher, she says we won't learn anything if we don't ask questions.'

Matron folded her thick arms beneath her bosom, which made it swell even further. It reminded me of blowing up balloons, those really big shiny ones, and then you release them and they go *ssplllrrrrrrrrrrrrrrr*, farting crazily in every direction. Suppose Matron's boobs were like that? The way she shoved her arms

under them and heaved away it looked like they might burst out of her jacket at any second and take off. Weapons of mass destruction, if you ask me. And now she stood there, flaunting them in my face while she studied a letter. She slowly leaned forward until her face was centimetres from mine.

'Felicity Foster-Thompson. Very high and mighty. You're the smart one, I suppose? There's always a smart one. Don't worry. It won't do you any good.' She straightened and gave me a shark-smile. I gave one back. My teeth, being mostly metal, are a lot more sharky than hers. She leaped back as if I'd actually bitten her, which I almost nearly did, but I'm a practising vegetarian. When I say 'practising' I mean I haven't actually started yet. I'm working on it. Do you think I say 'actually' too much? Anyway, when it comes to concealed weapons I have a surprise up my sleeve, or rather, in my mouth.

I noticed Matron was standing on a big doormat that had WELCOME printed across it. Ha ha ha. What a travesty. It should have said SHOVE OFF.

'Your skirt's too short,' Matron snapped.

'I can't help it. It's my long legs. If they were shorter the skirt would come further down.'

'Are you deliberately trying to annoy me, or are you congenitally stupid?'

I tried to look congenitally stupid, which isn't difficult when you've got fifty-thousand-year-old specs on.

I have found that looking stupid is the best means of defence when it comes to dealing with people over twenty, and Matron was well beyond. Her only hope of rescue now was a Time Lord.

I followed her in, and we were barely over the threshold when a giant with the most stupendous fungal growth under his nose came striding over.

'Major Trubshaw,' he boomed. 'You're late. Any particular reason?'

'Bus didn't come.'

'What bus? There isn't a bus that passes here.'

I sighed. 'So that explains it.' I tried to look congenitally stupid again.

Matron regarded me as if I was something horrible dragged off the street. Well, I had been dragged off the street, almost, but I'm not horrible. Not all the time, anyhow.

'This is Felicity Foster-Thompson,' muttered Matron, sucking in her cheeks. Why did she have to do that?

'Humph! How old are you?' growled the Major.

'Fourteen.'

'Are you indeed? What's all that muck on your teeth?'

'It's a brace. It's NHS. My parents won't allow me a proper one. I wanted an aqua-blue one like Sita's, which would be really cool, but my parents are, like, *so* Victorian, no, worse than Victorian, they're Tudor and they

said no way, which is why I have to go out like this, frightening the natives. Anyway, it's not muck, it's just a –'

'Stop!' cried the Major, holding up a hand. 'Stop right there, young lady! I asked you a simple question. I do not require your life history, your genealogy or anything other than a simple answer. There's one rule here and that is: always answer the question and nothing else.'

'That's three rules,' I pointed out, and the temperature in the room suddenly dropped by a few thousand degrees. Whoops!

'I beg your pardon?' said the Major.

'Matron says there are two rules and you say there's one rule, but they're not the same rule, so that makes three rules. So, there's . . . not . . . one rule . . . there are . . . three,' I said and I could hear my voice getting quieter.

Matron was flaring her nostrils at me and priming her weapons of mass destruction. The Major squeezed a ridge of flesh on his forehead with his fingers. Maybe it helped him think more clearly.

'Let's begin again,' he suggested. 'You take orders from Matron and myself. I think that makes everything perfectly clear.'

The Major flashed a gritted-teeth smile at me, as if he was daring me to challenge him. I guess that sometimes you have to play ball. Sometimes you meet someone who simply can't see how ridiculous they

seem to everyone else, especially me. Anyhow, keeping quiet had the desired effect, and the Major turned to the flint-faced Air-bags next to him. 'Good. Put her on tea duties, Matron.'

'Yes, Major.'

'When you've got the girl settled come and see me in my office. Another tablespoon has gone.'

'No!'

'Indeed. We shall have a full-scale search this time. Report back to me as soon as you can.' Off went the Major, marching down the corridor, left, right, left, right.

'What are you staring at, girl?'

'Nothing.'

'Good. Follow me.'

Matron led and I followed, quietly humming. 'Matron had a little lamb, its fleece was white as . . .'

'What's that?' hissed Matron. 'Don't speak unless you're spoken to, girl.'

I mouthed at Matron's back. As we passed a corridor I thought I saw a shadow move, and then it was gone. Eeek! A shiver went down my spine. I could see it all happening – *Fourteen-Year-Old Girl Found Dismembered and Eaten by Starving OAPs in House of Horror.*

Matron took me down into the bowels of the building, where there was a very small kitchen and a huge storeroom filled with cleaning materials. I have never seen so many buckets and mops and so on.

'First job is make tea. Trolley's over there. You need twelve cups and saucers, one for each of the residents, plus the Major and myself. When you've made the tea it goes on the trolley. Bring tea and biscuits to the Major and myself. Then take tea to each resident, one biscuit each. Avoid Mr Winkleberry in Room Seven.'

'What's wrong with him?'

'That's confidential,' Matron announced flatly. 'When you've seen to them you come back to us to collect our dirty crockery, then back to the residents to do the same, then down to the kitchen to wash up. Understood? Good. Get on with it.'

I made the tea and put a big pile of biscuits under a towel because I had decided to give the wrinklies two each. I am such a rebel. When I am mature, and have acquired bigger boobs and contact lenses and finished all my university courses and been made Top Scientist in the World, I am going to be a rebel, like Boudicca, only with a better dress sense. I mean, have you seen that statue of her in London? She's charging into battle, in a chariot, and she's gone topless! What kind of behaviour is THAT? I ask. Perhaps she was hoping to frighten the Romans. She should have taken Matron with her. Matron would have scared them witless. Mass panic.

Anyhow, I bet the residents would like an extra biscuit. The residents – who I hadn't even seen yet. Where were they all? I was in an old people's home

and I hadn't seen a single one. And then there was the mysterious Mr Winkleberry. What was that about?

I fed and watered Matron and the Major, who were deep in discussion about the Great Spoon Vanishing, which was obviously Hugely Important and would probably bring down the government and create chaos throughout known civilization like that butterfly in the rainforest. Then I set off to find some actual residents, and it didn't take long to find them, because they were all sitting in their rooms like they'd been told to go and stay there and not to come out until they were prepared to say sorry.

They were quite nice really and they weren't knitting coffins or falling to bits – well, not much, at any rate. Miss Dash's eye fell out a couple of times, but it was a glass one so I guess that was to be expected. I had to tell each one about Josh and me being on work experience. They were all smiles and so chatty, except for Mr Gumble, who'd lost his false teeth so I could hardly understand a word he said.

One lady wasn't in her room, so I didn't see her, and there was a French woman, Madame Dupont, who was lovely and smelled of flowers and looked ever so elegant and French, which isn't really surprising I suppose, seeing as she was. I told her I was going to study in Paris and become a famous scientist (and rebel) and she said she liked my skirt and she wasn't rude about it, like Matron. I told her what Matron had said.

'*Mais oui*, of course it's too short,' said Madam Dupont, seriously. 'That's the point, isn't it? And you look so *chic*. You are *très jolie*, you know, very pretty.'

Ha! That was something to tell Evie, who says I look like the Pink Panda. I said didn't she mean the Pink Panther? And she said no, she meant the Pink Panda and that's why she said it. According to Evie my prehistoric spectacles are like panda rings round my eyes. She's very supportive like that.

Anyway, I could feel myself go all hot. 'If you see a boy called Josh, will you tell him I'm pretty?' I begged. Madame Dupont laughed.

'This Josh. He is your boyfriend, *n'est-ce pas?*' She watched my face. 'Oh, I see. He is *not* your boyfriend. Not yet. Do not despair, *ma petite*.' She was tops – and she spoke French really well.

And they all liked their extra biscuit. I told them they mustn't choke or die or I'd be in big trouble and most of them said they were always in trouble anyway. Then I had to go and collect everything and wash it all up and by the time I'd done that I was totally exhausted and it was lunchtime and that was when I saw Josh for the first time. (I can't call him Goat. I know Charlie and all his friends call him Goat, but it's not very nice, is it? I mean, you wouldn't want to be standing at the altar in church with the vicar going: 'Do you take this Goat to be your lawful wedded husband?')

Josh couldn't see me because he was half turned

away and backing out of a storeroom with his arms full of toilet rolls for some strange reason and he looked so tall and strong. How can anyone carry a mountain of bog rolls and still look so gorgeous? It shouldn't be allowed. At least it should be allowed but only for me. I called to him and he was so surprised he dropped everything and toilet rolls went bouncing about all over the place. He whirled round and glared at me.

'Hi,' I said. I am so lame. Pathetic.

'Thanks a lot,' he grunted and began scrabbling for toilet rolls. I helped and crawled about on all fours thinking: this is romantic. I've always wanted to go on a toilet-roll hunt with my dream-boy. Although, actually, to tell you the truth, it was quite good because Josh was crawling about on all fours too and he has got the most hunky bum in the world. I could follow him to the ends of the Earth – well, at least as far as the end of the corridor, because my knees were getting sore. I told him it was lunchtime and we could go down the shops.

'Together?' he said.

'No, I thought I could go first and then you could creep out after me disguised as a giant yellow duck so nobody can recognize you and carrying a big sign that says I AM NOT WITH HER.'

'Are we allowed to go at the same time? That's what I meant. Have you met Major and Mrs Monster, the twin tubs?' I nodded meekly and felt terribly stupid.

'I'm hungry,' he muttered. 'I've been doing this all morning.'

'And I could murder a tortoise,' I said, and then thought: *I don't need to try and look congenitally stupid – I AM stupid!*

'You eat tortoises?' Josh looked blank.

'No, I just don't like them much,' I said weakly.

'Oh boy,' sighed Josh, as well he might, and we went out for lunch. He had a ham and mustard sandwich and I had egg and cress and he told me a joke and I laughed and he said I had a bit of sandwich stuck to my face. So I checked in my little mirror and discovered all these bits of cress caught up in my brace. It looked like I was growing mould all over my teeth. I had turned into a walking display of germ cultures. That was guaranteed to increase my charm rating by at least minus 100 per cent. And then I thought, hang on, he could really have made something of that. He could have told me I looked gross, because I did, but he just said I had something on my face. Maybe he secretly likes me!

Anyway, he went quiet after that and you know how, like, you think someone wants to say something, but they're sitting on it? It was like that, but not literally. I wanted to ask him but I reckoned just for once I'd shut up and wait and in the end he spoke.

'Did you meet Mrs Kowalski?'

'No, but I did meet Madame Dupont. She's French and quite cute really and she even said that . . .'

'Mrs Kowalski is weird,' Josh interrupted. 'She wears stealth slippers.'

'Stealth slippers?'

'That's what she calls them. You can't hear her coming. She appears suddenly from nowhere. I don't think Major and Matron like her.'

'That's because they don't like anyone.'

Josh stared at me. He seemed quite surprised. 'Do you think so? You could be right. Matron took Mrs Kowalski away to be searched.'

'Whatever for?'

'They thought she'd stolen a spoon.'

I recalled the Major's conversation with Matron earlier and asked Josh what kind of spoon.

'This kind,' said Josh, pulling a tablespoon out of his bag. I wasn't expecting that.

I didn't have a chance to give the spoon back to Mrs Kowalski. I had no idea what she was doing with it but it was obviously important and meant to be kept secret. I was swinging back to my first impression that maybe she was a bit mad or something. It was all too weird. I needed to talk but the only person available for listening was Fizz and I had no idea what she'd do or say. I don't think she has any idea of what she's going to do or say either.

Fizz is very strange. One moment she's talking like some demented crazy-creature, with bits of sense all mixed up with complete gibberish, and then she's staring at me with big eyes like she's never seen me before. Not to mention the skirt she was wearing. I don't remember seeing her in anything like that before and I'm sure I would have remembered. Maybe she wore something like it to the disco but I only had eyes for that floppy top. Her legs are quite something. Shame about the face. Big sis, Lauren, looks fantastic,

so I guess there were no genes left when it came to making daughter number two.

Fizz surprised me coming out of the storeroom this morning and I spilled all the toilet rolls. It had taken me five minutes to get that lot carefully balanced in both arms and she goes and jumps up behind me and I drop the lot. So she gets down on her hands and knees and starts helping me collect them together again and she's wiggling her behind at me. That's what it felt like but I don't suppose she realized. Anyhow, I'm not saying what I saw. So by way of returning the favour I showed her my spoon.

Fizz's jaw dropped. '*You* stole it!'

'Of course I didn't. Mrs Kowalski took it. Then Matron and the Major found us talking in the corridor and Mrs Kowalski stuffed it inside my trousers while they couldn't see. They accused her of taking it and took her off to be searched.'

Fizz was grinning from ear to ear. 'An old lady stuffed a spoon into your trousers? The dirty old baggage!'

'She's old enough to be Great-great-grandmother's great-great-grandmother. But I admit I was surprised.'

'Why did she take the spoon in the first place?'

'I don't know! Why do prunes steal spoons? Ask a psychologist, not me. Anyhow, I'll try and give it back to her this afternoon and find out a bit more. The thing is, I'm not very happy about the goons. That's what Mrs Kowalski says they called the guards in prison camps during the war. And that's just what the Major and Matron are like. They're control freaks. They run the place like a prison camp.'

'I know. And the worst thing is you're only allowed one biscuit.'

'What?'

'They told me I could only give the oldies one biscuit with their tea, but that is really mean, so I gave them two. That'll show 'em. Join the rebellion, brother.'

Fizz clasped a clenched fist to her chest. I think it was meant to be some kind of anarchist salute but she did it with such force she only made herself cough. I nodded. 'I guess that fits their general pattern of behaviour. I think Mrs Kowalski is up to something. She seems a bit dotty, but I don't think she is really.'

'Lots of people are like that,' smiled Fizz, showing her brace. At least all that cress had gone. I wondered what she meant when she said lots of people seem dotty, but aren't. Was she talking about herself?

'Why do you wear that?' I asked.

Fizz glanced curiously at her clothes and shrugged. 'What?'

'That brace.'

'To straighten my teeth – at least, that's what the dentist says, but everyone's got them, so what I think is either everyone's got crooked teeth or we've got crooked dentists.'

'How do you mean?'

'It's a scam by dentists to make pots more money for themselves and also they do it because they're jealous of our youth so they do everything they can to make us look ugly and horrible. Dentists are nasty people and not human. What do you get if you cross a sadist with a JCB? A dentist, that's what. Anyhow, we'd better be getting back before the Camp Commandant and Air-bags throw a wobbly.'

'Excuse me? Air-bags?' What was she on about now?

'Matron, you idiot. Have you seen the size of her chest? I reckon a couple of air bags have gone off under her jacket. She probably crashed into something when she was growing up and *whumpff*! Up they came and they've never gone down since.'

'Right.'

I avoided Fizz's eyes. This did not seem like a suitable conversation at all. Quite funny, though. Fortunately Fizz blithely ploughed on. She could talk for England. And Scotland. And Wales.

'What are we going to do about writing up the daily report for school? We're supposed to do it together. I think we should take it in turns – your house, then my house and so on.'

My heart fell into my shoes. 'Not a good idea,' I croaked.

'Why not? I know, your room's a mess. You're

ashamed of it. Doesn't matter. Wait until you see my room: it is the pigsty of all pigsties.'

'Sounds unmissable. Anyhow, my room is not a mess.'

'Really? I know, you've got posters of women all over your walls, haven't you?'

'No, I haven't!' I almost shouted and Fizz's eyes popped.

'Posters of men!' Fizz put a horrified hand to her mouth.

'NO!' I yelled.

'So what's the problem? Tell me.'

'Doesn't matter,' I said lamely, my mind in tatters. 'We'll take it in turns, but only if we start at your place.'

'OK,' Fizz agreed, just as we got back to Marigolds. 'See you later, Mystery Man.'

We went our separate ways. There was no sign of the Major but Matron was prowling the corridors like a Rottweiler.

'Bathrooms all done?'

'Yes.'

'Yes, Matron,' she corrected.

'Yes, Matron.'

'Are you smirking?'

'No, I've never smirked,' I said. 'It's a disgusting habit.'

Matron's eyes narrowed dangerously. She pursed

her lips, parted them as if to say something, thought better of it and pursed them again. 'The mail has arrived. You can take it to the room numbers marked on the envelopes. At three o'clock everyone meets in the garden room for afternoon tea. Miss Dash will need some help and so will Mrs Ogweyo. Help them into wheelchairs and bring them down in the lift. Well, don't just stand there. Get on with it.'

She handed over a small bunch of letters and I headed upstairs. I leafed through the envelopes and was surprised to see that every one had been opened. Matron was reading their private mail! By good luck there was one for Mrs Kowalski so I went straight to her room.

The old lady was sitting beside her window, gazing out at the view beyond. When she saw me she put a finger to her lips and beckoned. Then she whispered: 'I never know if the room's bugged or not.' In a louder voice she went on: 'Oh, thank you, is that the post? Thank you so much. Goodbye, dear.' Then she looked at me expectantly and I produced the tablespoon.

'Well done!' she whispered. 'I knew you wouldn't let me down. You see that corner of the carpet over there? If you pull it up carefully there's a loose floorboard. Hide it in there. Make sure you put the carpet back properly. You know, they came and searched my room this morning from top to toe but they never thought of

looking there. It was my husband who taught me tricks like that. Such a clever man.'

'Is he still . . . ?'

'Oh no, dear. He died thirty years ago. He flew twenty-six bombing missions, spent two years in a prison camp, and do you know how he died? He was hit by a bus.'

'Bummer. Sorry.'

'Yes. Is that what you say? "Bummer"? It does sound rather appropriate. I must try and remember it. I was upset at the time, of course. It seemed such a waste, but looking back on it now I'm pleased it was an unusual way to make his departure.'

'Is that how you got your name – Kowalski?'

'Yes. Jack's Polish parents emigrated to America after the First World War and Jack was born over there. Then came the Second World War and that was how we met. He flew bombers with the USAF and I flew Spitfires for the RAF.'

'Spitfires!' Oh yeah, right. Now we were entering Fantasy World, for sure.

'And Hurricanes, Mosquitoes and so on.' She saw the surprise on my face. 'It was a war. We had to get on with things.' Her eyes took on a far-away look. It was impossible to tell. Had she really flown Spitfires? Maybe I would be able to find out in due course, but I had a more pressing question to ask.

'What's so important about the tablespoon?'

Mrs Kowalski's head jerked up and she fixed her suddenly alert eyes on me. 'You won't tell, will you?'

'Of course not.'

'We're going to escape from here. We all are, every one of us. We're digging a tunnel, you see.'

Funk-hunk has been in my bedroom! He sat on my bed! Next to me! After he'd gone I lay across my bed and imagined he was still there, like my life-saving dream, only not so wet. He is, like, the Prince of Handsomeness. When we were working on our assignment he was leaning over me and I could feel the heat from his body and I was willing him to suddenly take me in his arms and sweep me off my feet and kiss me. Didn't work, unfortunately. I must learn mind control, then I could hypnotize him. *I have you in my power, Josh Cameron.* I could make him do anything. The mind boggles. Well, my mind does. I do quite a lot of boggling.

Josh stood by the window for a long time, staring out as if he could see some kind of supernatural vision or something, and I almost died. I mean, he looked so poetic and noble. It was impossible to concentrate on work. I just wanted to write I LOVE YOU across the screen a thousand times. Instead of which I had to write about Matron, the Major and old people trying to remember something that happened one minute ago and couldn't, but could remember where they were 12 February 1732. Completely bonkers.

After he'd gone I went down for supper and there they were – the Inquisition. (Not THE Inquisition, of course, because that's history. What I actually mean is my parents.) Mum and Dad were already at the table, and Lauren too, all dolled up as usual, with her impeccable make-up, flawless skin, full lips and proper set of boobs. Even her nose is straight, unlike Mum's, or Dad's or mine. (Sudden amazing revelation – maybe LAUREN ISN'T MY SISTER AT ALL! Maybe she was swapped at birth and Mum brought home someone else's baby and the real Lauren, my real sister, is out there somewhere and is actually a hideous, gap-toothed, zit-faced brat with a bumpy nose.)

'So that was Josh?' Mum said.

'No, it was Father Christmas,' I replied.

'No need to be rude,' murmured Dad.

'So "Father Christmas" is a rude word?'

'I think you know what I mean,' Dad went on.

'He's a perv,' said Lauren.

'What?'

'He's a perv,' she repeated.

I looked at her, then realized my mouth was hanging open, so I shut it quickly because I think that looks so stupid when someone stands there with their mouth hanging open. 'I don't think so,' I said curtly.

'He was standing at your window ogling me.'

'I don't think so,' I repeated, even more sharply.

'Fizz, he was there for ages. I was sunbathing and he stood there watching. I saw him through my sunglasses. Couldn't take his eyes off me.'

'Well, darling,' said Mum, 'if you were wearing that new blue bikini, I'm not surprised.'

'I felt like a cow at market,' Lauren declared, 'the way he was leering at me.'

'You're a cow, all right,' I muttered. I was furious, simmering, seething. How could she talk about Josh like that? That was so horrible. And how could Josh *behave* like that?! The swine! I'll kill him! I'll kill both of them!

'I don't think farmers leer at their cows,' Dad offered by way of a contribution to this edifying discussion.

'He was leering,' Lauren repeated.

'What I'm suggesting, Lauren, is that he was either looking at you as if you were a cow, or he was leering. I don't think he would be doing both.'

'All right!' yelled Lauren.

Mum patted Lauren's arm. 'I understand. I'm afraid that's men for you.'

'*I* don't leer,' Dad complained.

'You did when you were younger, darling,' said Mum sweetly. 'I distinctly recall you ogling me on many occasions. Don't huff and puff like that. I didn't mind, and Lauren shouldn't either. The poor boy's fourteen, what do you expect? He's probably never

seen so much flesh on display and, let's face it, Lauren, you were displaying it.'

'I was trying to get a sun tan . . .'

'. . . in the smallest possible bikini on this earth,' Mum finished for her. 'And why not? There's nothing wrong with that, particularly in your own garden. Just don't expect other people – especially men – not to notice.'

I was speechless. Dad tried to change the subject. 'How was Marigolds?'

'Zombie-land,' I sniped. 'And there's this huge woman, Matron, who runs the place like a prison camp. I'm sure she pumps herself up every day.'

'I think you'll find it's been scientifically established that it's not possible to pump someone up, at least not by much,' announced Dad, to all-round astonishment.

'Not by much!' squawked Lauren. 'How do you know? Have you been experimenting, Dad? That's disgusting.'

'Of course I haven't. I'm simply pointing out the fallacy behind Fizz's suggestion.'

I gave up. I didn't want anyone pointing out my fallacies, whatever they are. I crawled back to my room. All that time he'd been at the window Josh had been looking at my big sis. I'll kill him.

I rang Evie.

'What do you expect, Fizz?' she said. So sympathetic.

'It's tragic. Charlie's the same. The merest whiff of a low-cut top and his eyes are on stalks.'

'Are you talking about your low-cut tops or any old trout's?'

'Anybody's,' she growled. 'I mean, I want Charlie to see the inner me, my beautiful soul.'

'You'll have to take your shoes off then.'

'What do you mean? I am grievously trepidated that you are about to launch into one of your stupidly stupid jokes.'

'Shan't tell you then.'

'Go on,' Evie sighed wearily. 'I know I shall regret this beyond my afterlife.'

'If you take off your shoes you can show Charlie your sole.'

'Fizz,' Evie said slowly, 'I am coming round to your house to put you out of my misery.'

'OK, but what am I going to do? Goat lusts after big sis. How can I make him look at me instead of her?'

'Put a paper bag over Lauren's head?'

'Do you not think she might notice?'

'Not if you cut out two little holes for her eyes.'

'Now who's being stupidly stupid?'

'Hey, we could start a stupid club . . .'

'. . . and go round clubbing people!' we chorused and fell about laughing. That's Evie all over. What would I do without her? Become sane, probably. How awful.

After that I did some knitting. It takes my mind off

things. Very calming. I'm knitting a *thing*, which is what I usually knit. Evie and I do extreme knitting, which is, like, you get wool, whatever colour you feel like, and you knit and see how it comes out. You don't use a pattern because that makes it all predictable and we are freestyle, like, radicals at the forefront of knitting technology, developing our own style. I've done a shawly kind of *thing* and a belt *thing* and a scarf *thing*. They're brilliant. They look like something spun by a giant spider with two legs missing. I've got a pretty good eye for clothes. In fact that's what I'm going to be, I think – one of those people who goes through your wardrobe and says: 'Throw that out! Burn that! Cut that up! You should be wearing this fabulous brown corduroy bin liner.'

Of course, I shall have to wait until after I've completed all my university stuff and in-depth study of earwig pheromones. Not to mention my rebellion.

Report for Monday by Josh Cameron and Felicity Foster-Thompson

Monday

Marigolds is a care home for the elderly in Alopecia Avenue. It has ten residents. These are some of them:

Mrs Kowalski	*Weird, and quite possibly mad.*
Miss Dash	*Quite sweet. She has one leg, one eye and is mad-ish.*
Mrs Ogweyo	*Can't stop worrying. She talks all the time to Freddie, though we're not sure who Freddie is. She's obviously madder than mad.*
Madame Dupont	*French. Is she lost? Not mad. Elegant in a tottery kind of way.*

Fizz turned to Josh. 'Did Matron say anything to you about Mr Winkleberry?'

'Never heard of him.'

'She told me to avoid him. I wonder why? She said it was confidential.'

'I'd like to avoid all of them,' muttered Josh. 'Anyhow, what do you mean – "Elegant in a tottery kind of way"?'

'She walks like a model, but an old one.'

'Right, as if you'd know how models walk.'

Fizz got up and went to the end of the room. She stood quite straight, tipped up her chin and did a passable imitation of a model strutting her stuff, bearing in mind it was difficult to get into her stride because she could only do five or six paces before hitting the opposite wall, not to mention the fact that she had to wade through an ankle-high sea of discarded clothing, magazines, knitting, CDs and soft toys. 'See? That's what models do, but when Madame Dupont walks it's more like this.'

Fizz did the whole thing again, only this time she made her knees wobble so much she lost her balance and fell on to Josh. From there she slid to the floor. 'Whoops,' she grinned.

'How can you live in a mess like this?' he asked.

'Excuse me, I tidied up before I came out this morning.'

'Were you blindfold?' Josh wished he hadn't said that even as he listened to the words spilling out of his mouth. What would Fizz say when she saw his house?

Annoyed with himself, he went across to the window, while Fizz settled to work. In the garden Lauren was sunning herself in a bikini and sunglasses. Josh went hot and cold and hot again. She was perfect. She could be a film star, or a model – a far better model than Fizz would ever make. His heart thudded so hard he thought Fizz would hear. Was this what love felt like? He swallowed. Fizz looked up from the computer.

'You all right?'

'Yip,' he squeaked. 'I mean, yep.'

'Sounds like your voice is breaking,' teased Fizz. 'What's going on out there?'

'Nothing,' Josh squeaked again, wishing that something was, and tore himself away. He looked over Fizz's shoulder at what she was adding to the report.

The home is run by Major Trubshaw and Matron. Major Trubshaw has a loud voice and thinks everyone is deaf. This could be because he works with the elderly, although none of them appear to be deaf. He likes rules, but lets Matron carry them out while he stays in his room counting spoons. He seems to have a thing about spoons.

The residents are kept in their rooms for as long as possible and are only allowed out on special occasions, like Christmas, when they're given a biscuit. (Source of information – Miss Dash.) This is because of Matron, who is the biggest woman in history, quite probably. She is also completely bonkers. She behaves as if she's really in charge

but spends most of her time telling everyone off, especially us. She is not at all youth-tolerant.

The house is very big and has more staircases than a staircase factory. It smells of disinfectant, crap perfume and coffins.

'You can't put "crap",' said Josh.

'I already have. Anyway, it *is* crap.'

'And I bet you've never smelled a coffin in your life.'

'That's because you only get to smell a coffin at your death,' Fizz said smartly. 'It's what journalists call a bit of local colour. Mrs Taylor told us in English.'

'She's having an affair,' Josh informed Fizz.

'I know. Everyone knows. With her salsa tutor.'

'What on earth does he see in her? She's so mousy. She wears glasses.'

Fizz half turned and looked up at Josh. He was so gorgeous. Why did he have to be so dumb? 'I wasn't aware that wearing glasses stopped you from having a love life,' she said. 'Maybe Mrs Taylor's salsa tutor sees more of her than just her glasses.'

'I bet he does. A lot more!'

'That is not what I meant,' answered Fizz coldly. There was no point in pursuing it. She'd lost Josh to his fevered fantasy world. She turned back to the computer.

Today we had to make tea for all the residents and take it to their rooms. We had to climb up and down a hundred stairs about a thousand times. We also had to do cleaning and washing-up. We had to restock all the bathrooms. This took ages and ages and we hardly had any time for lunch and we were completely exhausted by the time we finished and we still had to write up this assignment. We think this stinks.

'I don't think we should put that,' said Josh.

'Why not? It does stink. In fact, it is downright execrable.'

'What's that supposed to mean?'

'It's worse than stinks. Don't you ever listen to Mrs Taylor? She said your friend Charlie's handwriting was execrable the other day and Charlie asked her what it meant. He's so cool.'

'Cool? Charlie?'

'Yeah, like sometimes he wears different socks – you know, his socks don't match. One time he had a red sock and a blue sock.'

'That's cool?' Josh asked in disbelief. Fizz rolled her eyes and sighed. Would Josh ever lighten up? Josh went on. 'If we're going to complain we should make it more . . .'

'. . . more what?' sighed Fizz. 'More complaining?'

'No. More like a proper complaint.'

Fizz sat back and stared up at Josh. 'What?'

'Let me do it,' Josh grunted, and he tried to push Fizz from her seat but she resisted. Him leaning up against her and pushing like that made her tingle. Josh gave a final shove and deleted Fizz's last sentence.

While we, the undersigned, accept that writing assignments and work experience are an unavoidable burden of school procedure we suggest that the work we are undertaking amounts to child labour and therefore places the school in grave danger of being pursued by the European Commission of Human Rights.

'Get you! Are you planning on becoming a lawyer?' demanded Fizz.

'I'm trying to be a bit more polite, that's all.'

'Basically what you've written is "It stinks", and you've used a thousand words when I used two. I still think two's better.'

'Maybe,' Josh answered, 'but mine will make a better impression on Mrs Taylor AND give us a better word count at the end.'

Fizz wrinkled her nose and nodded. 'OK, OK. Should we say something about the tunnel?'

'No,' said Josh. 'We don't know enough about it and I don't want to get Mrs Kowalski into trouble. She trusts me and I don't like the Major or Matron. They behave suspiciously. I think we should give the prunes all the help they need.'

Fizz's eyes sparked. 'Cool! The rebels strike back! How many words have we done? Mrs Taylor said we should do at least four hundred.'

'Three hundred and sixty-three.'

Fizz began typing again.

Number of words: Three hundred and sixty-three. This does not include the bit I just typed saying that the number of words is three hundred and sixty-three. If you include the bit that says three hundred and sixty-three words we have actually done four hundred and ten. Result! (Update – 411, not including this section in brackets.)

'I don't think Mrs Taylor will think much of that last bit,' sighed Josh.

'Tough. It's your turn tomorrow and we'll go to your house.'

Josh was silent. His house. Animals. Noise. Smell. Chaos.

Tuesday:
Compulsive Humour
Disorder

When I got back home from Fizz's there was a giant, hairy Alsatian guarding the front gate. I had to shout for Mum to come and restrain it.

'His name is Sheba,' Mum told me, trying to stop him lungeing at me. 'He just needs to get used to you.'

'Sheba's a girl's name.'

'He's confused.'

'You mean whoever named him is confused,' I answered, but Mum shook her head.

'Dogs often take on the character of their owner, you know, and sometimes exaggerate them a bit.'

I thought about that. 'So whoever named Sheba is a transvestite?'

'No, Josh, that's not what I meant at all. I shall think of a better name eventually – Tennyson, perhaps. Anyhow, where have you been?'

I told her. Mum raised her eyebrows and studied my face. I could hear the connections in her brain – click, whirr, clunk, thud. *My son has been at a girl's house. Aha!*

Boy + girl + house = relationship. It was tediously predictable.

'Felicity Foster-Thompson? Do I know her? What does she look like?'

That stumped me for a second. What *did* Fizz look like? My brain sifted possible answers at blinding speed.

Ans. No. 1. She wears the smallest miniskirt in school? Reject.

Ans. No. 2. She had blue knickers on today? Reject.

Ans. No. 3. She has fantastic legs? Reject.

Then I had it.

'She wears glasses and she knits.'

'Oh. Is she pretty?'

'No. She's got braces on her teeth, which she likes to tuck cress behind, and she's weird.'

'In what way?' asked Mum with interest.

How could I possibly describe what I meant by 'weird' to someone who thought keeping goats, snakes and iguanas in the house and naming them after poets was perfectly acceptable?

'She talks a lot,' I said at length.

'Oh, that *is* weird,' said Mum, giving me a disappointed look. 'Do you like her?'

'If you mean "like her" as in "like her", she's OK. If you mean "like her" as in "fancy her", the answer is "no".'

'I'll take that as a "yes" then,' beamed Mum.

'I said I don't fancy her!'

'Kids your age never say what they really mean. So how was Marigolds?'

'Full of loonies.'

The smile slid from Mum's face. 'Josh! They're old, that's all. They've lived more lives and have more memories than you and me put together. They may look decrepit to you but many of them have had extraordinary moments.'

So I told her about Mrs Kowalski flying Spitfires. Mum seemed to think that was way beyond extraordinary. 'Are you sure? I don't remember your great-gran ever saying anything like that. Women took on men's jobs when the men got called up but I've never heard of them flying. Great-gran was a Land Girl, working on the farm. But flying Spitfires?' Mum shook her head. 'Old people can get quite confused sometimes. She sounds a character, anyhow.'

I almost told Mum about the tunnel, but I sensed danger. Give an adult that sort of information and they are likely to do the sort of thing they would describe as 'sensible' – in other words, tell some authority or other, like the Department of Social Services Stop Tunnels for the Elderly. Besides, I didn't *have* any information, apart from what Mrs Kowalski had told me, and I wasn't entirely sure if I believed her. Mum thought the old lady was confused and she could well

be right. I decided to do a bit of research and went on the web. It wasn't long before I was directed to a possible site: www.motherflieshurricanes.com.

There it was in black and white. The ATA – Air Transport Auxiliary – was set up during the war for the RAF because of pilot shortage. Male pilots went on front-line service, while a whole flock of women pilots ferried new planes from factories to airbases, wherever they were needed. Mrs Kowalski must have been with the ATA. Maybe she *had* flown Spitfires. Cool.

I sat back in my chair and tried to take it all in. Battle. Prisoners. Tunnels. Flight. Escape. There were links here with my own life. The far end of my desk was dominated by the towering red fuselage of *Escape IV*. It was the fourth rocket I had built to my own design, and it was the biggest, the most complex and by far the most challenging one to construct. I was proud of it and now it was almost ready for its maiden flight. But would it work?

Why call it *Escape IV*? Because one day I would be an astronaut. I would leave this animal house, this mad world, and fulfil my dream of going to the stars. Dad's dream too, but he was too old now, unless somebody was planning to build an interplanetary care home somewhere up there. I was sure Mrs Kowalski would understand my dream of flying, just as I understood her dream of escaping.

But before any of these dreams could be fulfilled I had to remove three jungle frogs from the shower and get cleaned up after working at Marigolds. It was only when I was showering that I noticed a small green snake coiled around the shower head, watching me. Milton had escaped again. I got dressed, wound him round a finger and wearily returned him to his vivarium. Still, it was good to feel clean again after all that contact with prehistory.

All I had to do now was worry about bringing Fizz back to the house. My bedroom was fine – clean and neat as always – unless some creature decided to wander in and make their nest, den, lair, eyrie or burrow in my room while I was out. It was the rest of the house I was worried about. Suppose Fizz needed the loo and came face to face with Milton? He wasn't poisonous, but how would Fizz know? It wasn't as if he had a label round his neck.

'He likes being near water,' said Mum.

'Why not put a bowl in his tank then?'

'Because animals don't expect to find water next to them. It's not natural. They must hunt for it. It's an instinct. They have to go on a search. Same as us. We're all animals, and we're all searching, Josh.'

I think that was Mum's Thought For The Day. I wondered what I was searching for. That was easy. Lauren. However, at the moment I had more pressing things on my mind. Perhaps I could tidy up the house

a bit? Or perhaps not. How can you tidy up five goats, two hamsters, a gerbil, four guinea pigs, two rabbits, three dogs, five cats, a pigeon and an eagle owl? Not forgetting Milton.

I rang Charlie. He's working in a shoe shop and I asked him how it was going.

'Goat, you really don't want to know. In a word, socks. You wouldn't believe the state of some people's socks. Not to mention their feet.'

'Their feet?'

'I told you not to mention them.'

'That bad?'

'Yes. How did it go at the care home?'

I told him about Mrs Kowalski flying Spitfires.

'Cool! Has she got a moustache?'

'What?'

'I thought you had to have a big, bushy moustache to fly Spitfires. You look at the photographs of flying aces. They have all got big, bushy moustaches.'

'Charlie, you're an idiot.'

'My great-gran had a moustache. I remember it clearly.'

'Mrs Kowalski does not have a moustache. Listen, I saw Lauren this afternoon.'

'Don't say that word. I shall have to lie down in a dark room.'

'She was sunbathing in a blue bikini.'

'Oh God.'

'And she was rubbing sun oil on.'

'OK, that's enough. I can't cope. I'm putting the phone down.'

And he did. I'd meant to ask him how I could wriggle out of the next day's appointment with overwhelming embarrassment, namely Fizz coming to my house, but it was too late now, and by the time I went to bed I still hadn't thought of a way out of it.

I didn't sleep well. I had a dream about Lauren. She was here visiting and she was looking at all the animals. She thought they were cute, until one of the jungle frogs jumped down her front and she screamed. She stood there waving her hands frantically, not daring to do anything because she thought the frog was venomous and might bite her. She kept screaming at me, 'Get it out! Get it out!' I had to put my hand down her top but the frog kept jumping about. It was really difficult to get hold of and I'd make a grab and get something else instead and Lauren kept on yelping. Eventually I managed to pull it out and put it back in the tank only to have Lauren collapse into my arms sobbing. 'You saved me!' she said. There was a bit more after that. Little wonder I didn't sleep well.

Then I had to drag myself off to Marigolds for another day piling up loo rolls and delivering them and all that kind of stuff. It was so boring. At least until Fizz showed up. She was late again of course and she

got another roasting from Matron. She was so fed up she abandoned all the washing-up and slipped upstairs to see what I was doing. There's no stopping her. She pokes her nose into everything.

'These bathrooms are unreal,' she said. 'What is all this stuff for?' I stopped my exciting work replacing bars of soap and went over to where she was inspecting a big metal arm that stuck out from the wall. Four steel hawsers hung from the arm, attached to a floppy seat.

'What do they do in here?' winced Fizz. 'Suspend wrinklies by their thumbs?'

'It's a hydraulic hoist for people who are unable to get into the bath by themselves.'

'Cool! How does it work then?'

'You fill the bath and sit in this little seat. These are the controls. Lift, swing across over the bath and lower yourself into the water. Job done.'

Fizz beamed at me. 'Great! Let's do it! Get in the seat.'

'Fizz!'

'Oh, lighten up, Josh. I'm bored to death. Go on, get in.'

I admit I was curious too. I sat in the seat. Fizz pressed a button and I landed heavily on the floor.

'Oops! Sorry. I've just noticed – it says DOWN beside that button.'

'Try UP,' I said, trying not to sound too sarcastic.

The machine hummed. I slowly rose into the air. The seat swung from side to side. The machine whirred and I moved across to the bath.

'I wonder if it has an EJECT button,' mused Fizz, then saw the look on my face. 'It's a joke. OK, let's get you washed. Of course, you should get undressed first.'

That was when Matron burst in. 'Oh no you don't! I heard that, young lady. What on earth do you two think you're playing at? You wait until your school hears about this, not to mention your parents. They will be appalled. I blush to think what you might have done next.'

'It was a joke,' explained Fizz. 'I meant that if Josh was really going to have a bath he would need to get undressed but obviously he wasn't going to have a real bath so he wasn't going to get undressed either. I was teasing, wasn't I, Josh?'

I nodded glumly as the seat swung above the bath, with me trapped in it. I felt such an idiot. Matron's Kalashnikov eyes were still spraying bullets in every direction.

'And just what did you think you were doing playing with this equipment?'

'We're practising for when we're old,' Fizz answered brightly. I groaned inwardly. Didn't Fizz have any sense of self-preservation at all?

'Don't talk nonsense, and you, boy, get out of that

seat at once. Do you think this equipment is a toy? It's hugely expensive. How dare you behave like this. Wait until your head teacher hears about it. I said, get out!'

I was still struggling in mid-air. Just as I was carefully sliding out of the seat Fizz pressed the DOWN button and I was dumped in the bath. 'Ow!'

Matron hauled me to my feet. 'Wait for me outside the Major's office,' she hissed. 'Both of you.'

Fizz and I trooped downstairs. 'Congratulations,' I growled.

'It's your fault,' she said. My jaw hit the floor and bounced back up.

'What? How do you make that out?'

'If you hadn't been upstairs I wouldn't have come up to find you and I wouldn't have found the bathroom and if you hadn't got into that seat it wouldn't have happened at all.'

'But you told me to get in.'

'Maybe, but you didn't have to. If you hadn't got in it wouldn't have happened.'

'You mean if I hadn't been there none of this could have happened?'

'Yes.'

'On that basis it would be better if I hadn't even been born,' I pointed out coldly.

'Yes.'

'In fact, logically, that means that it would be better

if my parents hadn't been born, then they couldn't have produced me. And their parents shouldn't have been born either, or their parents, or their parents, all the way back to Adam and Eve.'

'That's right,' said Fizz with a curt nod. 'It was all their fault. Adam and Eve's.'

'Try telling the Major that,' I said and I couldn't help smirking.

And you know what? She did! Was he impressed? Not a bit of it. He told her she was being ridiculous. But I was impressed, which was strange. It was as if I had dared her and she'd accepted. I don't know what it is with Fizz. She's like one of those itches you get in the middle of your back that you can't quite reach. Annoying.

I think the Major would have let us go with a telling-off but Matron went on and on and made such a fuss about 'abusing expensive equipment' that in the end the Major made us stay in at lunchtime and do extra work to make up for the time we'd spent 'playing', as he put it. Then, in the afternoon, I was surprised by Mrs Kowalski again, creeping up on me in her stealth slippers.

'How's the tunnel going?' I asked.

'We've had a fall. What was that word? Oh yes – a bummer. Some of the roof came down last night. That's the problem with tunnels. It's difficult to find roof props. Zimmer frames are the best. My husband

told me how to do it. Jack knew, you see. He'd worked on two in the war.'

'Two?'

Mrs Kowalski nodded proudly. 'He was shot down and ended up in a POW camp. He joined an Escape Committee and they tunnelled out, six of them. Four got away but Jack and a friend were recaptured. Later they tried again, and then the war finished. He talked about it a lot, told me how they did it. Now it's our turn.'

'I thought you were digging it on your own?'

Mrs Kowalski shook her head. 'Oh no. I couldn't do it by myself. Madame Dupont is helping me. She's French, you know.' I nodded and Mrs Kowalski went on. 'She was in the Resistance during the war, getting escaped prisoners out of France and blowing up ammunition trains. That sort of thing.'

'Cool!'

'Oh yes. I don't suppose you could get me a spade? It would help so much with the digging.'

'How do I get it into the building?'

'You must think of something,' said Mrs Kowalski. 'Use your noddle. There's a war on.' She winked at me and slipped silently back into the shadows.

Great. More problems. Smuggle a spade into Marigolds. As if wondering what to do about Fizz coming back to my house wasn't enough. How was I going to get out of that? Life in all its glory. And then it came to me.

Late again this morning. Air-bags had a good go at me, but I was way ahead of her and had my excuse ready. 'The taxi didn't turn up,' I explained.

'Why not?'

'I hadn't ordered one.'

Well, I thought it was funny. Hey, it was, come on! When I know I'm in trouble I have this dreadful compulsion to tell jokes. I guess I'm trying to make people laugh and forget about what I've done. The problem is, I can't remember it ever actually working and it didn't work this time either. But then anything I said to Matron was bound to be wrong, so in for a penny, in for a pound.

'I'll have to tell the Major,' she said, when quite clearly she didn't have to at all. She was enjoying getting me into trouble. And why did she keep threatening me with her air-bags? I shrugged. What else could I do? Beg for my life? The morning was turning into a complete disaster zone and I was the centre of it.

After lunch I went off to find Madame Dupont. She always cheers me up.

'How I wish I were young again.' That's what she said when she saw me.

'Why do people say that?' I asked. 'I want to be older.'

'And when you get older you want to be younger. We are never satisfied. But I see you now and I wish I could dress like you, with your miniskirts and your short-cut tops. I bet all the boys stare at you.'

'Huh!'

'Oh! *C'est Mademoiselle Mécontente!*' She laughed and patted my arm, then translated, thank goodness, because my French is just the same as the French they have in France – incomprehensible. 'Miss Grumpy. So, why the long face? Is it that boyfriend of yours?'

'That's the trouble. He's not my boyfriend. I wish he were, but I think he's in love with someone else.'

'*Ooh là là!* That is sad. Who is she, this little minx that has your boyfriend's heart?'

'My sister. Lauren.'

'*Ooh là là!*' repeated Madame Dupont.

'She's seventeen,' I added pithily, and Madame Dupont sighed deeply. As well she might.

'She's seventeen and has proper boobs, not little squashed things like Yorkshire puds that have gone wrong, and she's . . . she's . . . really beautiful!' I burst out.

Madame Dupont folded me in her arms and held me tight while I tried so, so hard not to cry, and I

didn't. She rocked me back and forth and it was like she could feel my heart thundering away and she was waiting until it all went calm. Finally she let go and looked carefully at my face. She took off my glasses and wiped away the tears I was sure I hadn't cried and studied me again.

'But he is mad,' she murmured. 'There is no doubt. He is mad. You are a beautiful girl and soon you will be a beautiful woman and don't let anyone tell you anything different. You have spirit. Isn't that why they call you Fizz?'

'Actually, it's short for Felicity,' I explained, and Madame Dupont shook her head.

'No, no. It's Fizz because you are so fizzy,' and she laughed, and when she said it like that, with her French accent, it sounded so good, so cool. It made me smile.

'I must have words with your boy,' said Madame.

'Don't tell him I told you!'

'Of course not,' she snapped back. 'But I think maybe you – he – you both need a little help.'

'Such as?'

'I have absolutely no idea whatsoever,' said Madame, and we both burst out laughing. 'Maybe you have some time together on your own?'

'We have to write a daily report for school. We're going back to his house this afternoon.'

'Good. Then pay him some attention. Don't tell him how handsome he is, or that you love him. If you say those things he will vanish for sure, *fwitttt*, like an Olympic runner. Tell him he looks tired. Rub his back for . . .'

'. . . a massage!' I cried. What a brilliant idea. That was something I could actually do. My mum does run a beauty parlour, after all.

'Yes,' said Madame Dupont. 'I think that will help him forget your sister.'

'He's going to be blown away!'

'You be gentle with him,' she warned. 'Take it slowly.'

I could hardly wait to start and the rest of the afternoon was such a drag. It came to an end at last and Josh and I set off for his house.

'So where exactly do you live?' I asked.

'I had a good idea,' he said, striding ahead. 'We'll go to the library to do the project.'

'The library!'

'Yes. Then if we need to look anything up, we can.'

'The library?!'

'Yes. Come on.'

I stopped dead. All my plans were being piled on the bonfire and were about to go up in flames. I had to stop this somehow. I pulled at his arm.

'We can't,' I said.

'Why not?'

'We can't because, because, because I've been banned.'

'You've been banned from the library? What did you do?'

Good question. I desperately tried to think of a good answer to go with it.

'I made a noise.'

'You don't get banned for making a noise. Don't talk rubbish.'

He turned to go and I yanked at his arm again. 'I did. I made a noise and I got banned.'

'Oh yeah, right. So what sort of noise got you thrown out?'

'I screamed.'

Josh just looked at me. I could see he didn't know whether to believe me or not, and I'm not surprised because I didn't believe me either.

'They wouldn't throw you out just because you screamed,' he said.

Huh! What would he know? This was making me cross and I grabbed his arm again. 'Listen, Mr Know-All, I screamed, right? I saw a mouse and I screamed. It ran out from under a huge, ginormous bookcase – you know, like they have in libraries –'

'Yeah, yeah, I know libraries have bookcases,' growled Josh.

'Right, and it was huge, this bookcase, and the mouse ran out and I leaped back and banged straight

into an old man and then we both fell back against another ginormous bookcase and it toppled over and hit another bookcase and the two went down kind of like dominoes, right? Big mess. Horrendous. Books everywhere. So I got banned.' I looked at Josh to see if he'd bought it.

'What happened to the mouse?' he asked.

'What mouse? Oh, the *mouse*! It escaped.'

Josh looked really tired now. Great.

'I'm not allowed in,' I added, in case he hadn't got the message. 'I'm sorry, but it doesn't matter. We can go to your house, like we planned.'

'I can't believe I'm working with someone who got thrown out of a library.'

'I know,' I said. 'It's quite an achievement really. They should give me a certificate, or a badge, you know, like when you're a Girl Guide.'

'I've never been a Girl Guide.'

'Shame,' I said. 'That was the one thing missing from Girl Guides.'

'What was?'

'Boys. Now, which way to your house?'

Report for Tuesday by Josh Cameron and Felicity Foster-Thompson

Josh had a brainwave. Dad. They'd go to his dad's house. Josh had his own key and Dad would still be at work. It was only a couple of streets away and it was clean, tidy and quiet. Nobody would be there. It was perfect. He couldn't believe he hadn't thought of it before. A wave of relief swept through him. The only problem now was that they had to walk down his own road and past his real home to get to Dad's. He hoped Mum wouldn't spot them. It was a risk he'd have to take. He crossed his fingers.

As they passed his house Sheba lunged at the gate and barked furiously. One of the goats stared out at them from the front-room window.

'Hey!' cried Fizz. 'That must be where Wacky-Woman lives.'

Josh cringed. Wacky-Woman. Was that what they

called his mother? His face flushed with shame and anger. Wacky-Woman? He jumped to her defence.

'All she does is look after strays and sick animals. Somebody has to.'

'Yeah, but she's weird,' laughed Fizz. 'And she's a lezzie.'

Josh stopped dead and shouted. 'You are SO STUPID. You don't know anything, do you? You just shout your mouth off saying stupid things.'

Fizz took several steps back, eyes wide. 'OK, OK, it's a joke, all right?'

'No, because jokes are funny and that wasn't, it was sick. You can't just say things about people that aren't true. Suppose someone believes you?'

'That's why it's a joke,' Fizz hit back. 'Nobody believes a joke.'

'OK, so suppose, just suppose, that someone says your mum is a lezzie. How would you feel about it?'

'I'd think they were stupid, because she isn't.'

Josh folded his arms and looked at her. Fizz stared back at him. A faint flush came to her cheeks and she frowned momentarily. 'OK, I'm stupid, but she is definitely weird. I mean, did you see that goat looking at us? It was in the front room.'

'So?' Josh started walking again, rather pleased with himself.

Fizz trailed behind. 'I really don't get you,' she called after him. 'Sometimes you're completely uptight

and straight and then you act like goats in the front room are OK.'

'I don't think it's anything to worry about. She's doing a proper job looking after sick animals. What's wrong with that?'

'Not in the front room! You don't put goats in the front room!'

Josh stopped. 'Why not?' he snapped.

'Because that's where you put the television, stupid.'

Josh burst out laughing. 'You are something else,' he said. 'That takes the biscuit, that does. You can't put a goat in your front room because that's where the telly goes? Is that what you're saying?'

'No. No, not only the television, but lots of reasons like, like they might do a whoopsie on the carpet and they might want to sit on the armchairs and the sofa and leave their hairs all over the place and before you know it they'll be putting their feet up on the coffee table and eating TV dinners and snatching the remote control and demanding to watch boring animal programmes and soon they'll be taking over the whole house and sleeping on your bed and they'll probably mate and have lots of little goats and then they'll throw you out of house and home and before long they'll have formed the next government and taken over the world and the world will be ruled by goats.' Fizz looked up at him and smiled. 'No offence, Goat.'

Josh was astonished. Apart from a bit of exaggeration here and there Fizz had painted an almost complete picture of life in his house. He couldn't think of an answer. And the way she called him Goat at the end made him realize something else. Everyone at school, even Charlie, called him Goat. But hearing Fizz emphasize it like that made him aware that she'd never called him Goat. She always called him Josh. He was confused. 'Come on, let's get on so we can write up this wretched project.'

Fizz didn't think much of what she assumed was Josh's house. It was empty and lifeless. There was nothing on the walls. It was all too clean, like those demonstration rooms in furniture stores – the kind of room where you die of boredom within twenty seconds.

'They ought to put the wrinklies in here,' she muttered.

'Why?'

'It would put them out of their misery. They'd give up the will to live and die on the spot.'

Josh found himself surprised, again. He'd never found anything wrong with Dad's house. Maybe it was because he needed a strong antidote to his own home. He liked coming here, to the peace and quiet, where he knew where everything was because it didn't get eaten by goats or buried by dogs or sat on by sleeping tortoises. He went to the computer.

Tuesday

Today we did the same as yesterday. Is this what the wonderful world of work is like? At school every new day is much like the day before. Go to lesson. Break. Go to lesson. Lunch. Go to lesson. Games. Go home. At Marigolds it's like this: Put out soap and toilet rolls. Make tea. Break for tea. Do washing-up. Put out more soap. Clean baths and basins. Lunch. Clean more baths and basins. Do more washing-up. Put out toilet rolls. Go home. Day after day.

We do not feel that the experience of work experience we are experiencing is particularly beneficial. When we leave school we are not going to work in an old people's home. Felicity is going to be a singer in an all-boy band (somehow), and I am going to work in space.

'You're a girl,' Josh said. 'How will you get into an all-boy band?'

'You're so picky, aren't you? I could have a sex-change operation. What about you then? An astronaut? In your dreams! Building a rocket, are you?'

Josh opened his mouth and closed it. He'd almost said yes, he was. But he didn't. He didn't trust her, especially after the things she'd said about his mother.

'Listen, by the time I'm in my twenties space travel will be normal. Lots of people will do it and anyone who goes into space is an astronaut. That's where I want to work. Out there, among the stars.'

'Cool,' said Fizz, and went quiet. She stood behind him and they both stared at what Josh had written. Josh's brain seemed to congeal inside his skull. He couldn't think of any more. Fizz gazed over his shoulder. She wanted to put her hand in his hair and ruffle it up, but didn't dare. She remembered her conversation with Madame Dupont.

'You look tired,' she suggested.

'Really?' Josh was taken aback, because it was true, he was tired. He felt her hands on his shoulders. She began kneading, digging her thumbs and fingers into the flesh above his shoulder blades. Surprise gave way to submission. Behind his back, Fizz smiled. Her thumbs worked on the base of his neck. Josh lowered his head and closed his eyes.

'Good?' she murmured, after a couple of minutes.

'Mmmm. Where did you learn how to do that?'

'Mum does it to all of us – me, Dad, Lauren.'

'Ow!'

'Sorry,' Fizz said quickly. Speaking her big sister's name had made her lose concentration for a second. She wanted to ask Josh about Lauren and had to press her lips together hard and remind herself of what Madame Dupont had said.

'We've got to finish this report,' muttered Josh.

Fizz stopped. 'OK, my turn, shove your bum off that seat.'

Here are some of the surprising things we have learned while working at Marigolds.

1. *The only dishwasher they have is me. You really would expect a twenty-first-century home catering for a large number of people to have a dishwasher, wouldn't you? What is wrong with them? Are they so stingy they think they can't afford one? If they bought one they would save money because they wouldn't have to pay me – not that they do pay me, which they jolly well should – but they have to pay the person who normally washes them when they are not taking advantage of the slave labour provided by the local schools Work Experience programmes.*

2. *The staff of Marigolds do not seem to like us trying to broaden our knowledge of working with old people. For example, Josh and I spent part of the morning trying to familiarize ourselves with the workings of the hydraulic bath hoist. Instead of praising our efforts we were chastised . . .*

Josh couldn't help laughing. 'Chastised? Where on earth did you get that from?'

'Mrs Taylor, of course. She's good on words.'

> *. . . by the staff and told to get on with far less interesting work. How can we possibly learn anything in such an environment?*

'You're giving your vocabulary a bit of a workout,' Josh admired. Fizz blushed.

'I remembered what you said yesterday, when you complained about my writing being crap and you rewrote it and made it sound all flowery.'

Now Josh reddened. 'I didn't say it was crap. It was only some of the words you used.'

'Exactly, so now I have given you "chastised" and "environment". I'll check the number. Three hundred and thirty-four. What else can we put?'

'It would be really good to say something about Mrs Kowalski and the tunnel but it might get her into trouble, me too after hiding that spoon for her. Which reminds me, she wants me to get her a spade. How am I going to smuggle a spade into Marigolds? I'll never get it past Air-bags.'

'I'll do it,' offered Fizz. 'There's one in the shed. It only ever gets used once in a blue moon.'

'How will you do it?'

'I'll think of something.'

Josh didn't doubt it. If there was one thing Fizz was good at, it was thinking up hare-brained ideas, like trying out bath-hoist equipment for example. He gazed down at the computer screen, wondering what else they could write.

'The trouble is, all the wrinklies do is sit in their rooms all day and . . . wait a sec!'

'What? What?'

'I've had an idea. Let me,' said Josh, squeezing on to the seat beside Fizz.

It is clear that life in an old people's home is very boring, and so is our work, so we have decided that tomorrow we are going to use our initiative and organize something for the residents to do.

'Really?'

'Why not?' asked Josh.

'What sort of things?'

'Games.'

'What sort of games?'

Josh threw his arms up in despair and managed to send Fizz flying off the edge of the chair. She sprawled on the ground. 'Sorry,' he said, offering a hand and pulling her back up. 'Look, I don't know what sort of games. I was trying to write some extra words and it just came to me. I think it's a good idea.'

'Maybe it is a good idea, but it would be even gooder if we knew what the games were going to be.'

'You can't say "gooder". It's not a proper word. You mean "better".'

'It was a joke.'

'Oh, right. One of your jokes again.'

'What do you mean by that?'

'Only that your jokes aren't very jokish sometimes.'

'You can't say "jokish". "Jokish" is not a proper word. Hah! Up yours!'

They began pushing each other until Fizz fell over again and in the heat of battle Josh instinctively leaped on her and pinned her down. For a moment their eyes blazed at each other, then Josh was engulfed by embarrassment and jumped off.

'So that's how you treat a girl,' said Fizz with half a smile as she lay on the floor.

'I'm going to finish this,' Josh grunted.

We hope to provide them with something that they will all want to take part in.

'That's three hundred and eighty-nine. Eleven words short. Oh God, my brain's dead.'

'I'll do it,' said Fizz, getting up from the floor.

We are looking forward to putting our ideas into action and will report back on it tomorrow.

'There. Four hundred and six words. Done.' She sighed. 'Hurrah. I'd better be off home.'

'Me too,' said Josh and his heart fell out of his mouth.

'What do you mean? You live here, dead-brain.'

Josh forced a grin. 'I know. Just forgot. I'm tired.' Then, as he saw Fizz to the door his father arrived back from work.

'Wasn't expecting to see you today, Josh. What are

you doing here? Are you off back to your place? How's your mother?' He eyed Fizz and his face darkened a fraction. 'Who's this? You haven't been using my house for hanky-panky, have you?'

The questions came thick and fast and now two people were watching Josh and waiting for answers.

Wednesday:
What to Do with
Wheelchairs

I've been massaged. There's a first time for everything I guess. It was . . . unexpected. Fizz only did my shoulders but it felt like she touched all of me until I tingled. She said that there are particular places on the body that link to other parts of the body. (As if I didn't know.) And when she touched them it would affect other areas. Which it did. Not that I told her. Anyhow, she might do it again. That'd be good.

She knows I live somewhere else. I had to tell her, although I did leave out one or two details, like umpteen cats, dogs, goats, frogs, plus, as of yesterday, a donkey. ('I've called him Wordsworth,' Mum told me. 'I've always thought Wordsworth was a bit of a donkey.' I didn't ask her which bit.) But I had to promise that we'd go to my house on Thursday. That gives me less than forty-eight hours to think up something. Maybe I could use Yellow Pages and ring up a house-cleaning service, but really what I need are zoo cleaners. There wouldn't be much point anyway because it would all be dirty and covered in hair

again within seconds. What bugs me most is why do I care? What does it matter if Fizz sees where I live? It's that itch in my back again. Annoying. Doesn't make sense.

Dad was hilarious when he caught Fizz and me leaving his house. Actually he was boring and embarrassing at the time. It was only later when I was telling Charlie that I realized it was funny.

'He really thought you and Fizz had been up to something?' Charlie guffawed.

'Exactly. I mean, Fizz of all people.'

'Oh, I dunno, Goat. I reckon she's OK.'

'You're having me on.'

'No. More to her than meets the eye, I reckon.'

'Maybe it's what meets the eye that's putting me off – like that mouth.'

'Yeah but, you know, there's more to a mouth than just teeth, isn't there?'

'What are you on about, Charlie?'

'OK, I know there's the teeth, Goat, but there's also lips and tongue and all that. It's all mouth-stuff, isn't it?'

'What are you going on about, Charlie?'

'I'm not sure. Ask me tomorrow. I may have figured it out by then.'

That's typical Charlie. He gets some vague idea that he tries to put into words and the more he tries the faster the idea evaporates. Anyway, he's supposed to

be head over heels with Evie but he was talking like he fancied Fizz. Very odd.

Fizz was pretty surprised by what Dad was suggesting too. She thought the idea was so crazy she laughed in his face.

'You think I'm with him? You've got to be joking. I've got a proper boyfriend and it's not him. If you must know, we've been writing up our work experience report.'

'Exactly,' I agreed. 'Anyhow, Fizz isn't my kind of girl.'

'No. He prefers older women,' she said and looked at me with one eyebrow raised, like she knew something. Whatever, it made me blush because it brought Lauren to mind, in her blue bikini. It's horrible how your brain suddenly throws these things up at inappropriate moments.

Dad seemed satisfied with Fizz's explanation and said we could work there again if we wanted but to ring him and make sure he was in first. 'It's not that I don't trust the pair of you,' he explained. 'It's because . . .'

'. . . you don't trust us,' I finished for him. At least he smiled.

'Yes, sort of. It is my house, and I know what I was like at your age.' He grinned. Sometimes your parents can give you too much information.

'It's OK,' said Fizz. 'I'm not going to molest him

and it doesn't matter because we'll be going to his mum's house next time.'

This time it was Dad's eyebrows that went up. Perhaps he saw the panic on my face. 'I expect you'll find that very interesting,' he muttered and left it at that. But it still means I have to take Fizz back to my place on Thursday, unless I can think of a way out. Maybe I should dig a tunnel. Or even better, I could use Mrs Kowalski's tunnel to break *into* Marigolds. I could hole up there!

Fizz wanted to know why I'd pretended in the first place.

'It's a bit noisy at my house, that's all.'

'I thought you lived on your own, I mean with your mum – the two of you?'

'Yes.'

'So what's with the noise? I know! I bet your mum sings, doesn't she? Opera – she sings opera. She does that wobbly, howly stuff, doesn't she? Ooee-ooee-oo.'

'No, Fizz, she doesn't, and if she did sing like that she'd have to be put down.'

'Well, what then? She plays drums? The tuba? Yeah – I bet she's a secret tuba player!'

'NO!'

She suddenly danced in front of me so she could stare into my face, big-eyed. 'It's not something funny, is it? Do you quarrel or something? Does she hit you?'

‘NO!’

‘I know, you hit her!’

‘Will you shut up?’

‘I want to know!’

‘You want to know what my mum does?

‘Yeah.’

‘You really want to know?’

‘Yeah!’

‘She writes poetry.’

Fizz was stunned and stopped dead. ‘She writes poetry?’

‘Yes.’

‘That’s not noisy.’

‘I never said it was.’

‘What are they about then, her poems?’

‘Animals, mostly.’

‘Cool! You mean like “Tiger, tiger, burning bright” – stuff like that?’

‘I can only remember one about stick insects.’

Fizz stopped again. ‘Stick insects? How can you possibly write a poem about stick insects?’

‘Don’t you ever stop asking questions?’

‘Mrs Singh says if you don’t ask . . .’

‘Yeah, I know what Mrs Singh says.’

‘How did it go then?’

‘I can’t remember but it was called “The Stick Insect’s Dream”, and the creature is saying how it longs to eat more, become fat and turn into a log insect.’

‘That is so funny!’

‘It’s stupid,’ I muttered.

‘No, it’s really funny. I can’t wait to meet your mum.’

My heart torpedoed my trainers. Fortunately we had reached the end of her road by this time and I said I’d see her the next day. Off she went, trailing her bag down the street. Strange creature. Great legs, though.

Anyhow, we had quite a good time today at Marigolds. Fizz was late, but that’s so normal now Matron didn’t even bother to tell her off. She just gave a deep sigh and told us we were to switch duties and Fizz would do what I’d been doing and I’d take on her tasks.

‘I can’t wait,’ said Fizz, while Matron looked at her, trying to decide if she was being facetious or not. We all know the answer to that. I don’t think Fizz can do ‘serious’. I think she’s got a humour default setting in her brain or something. Wonder who her boyfriend is? Only an oddball would go out with her.

I didn’t see Fizz for a couple of hours, I was so busy making tea and so on. At least it was a change from toilet rolls and soap. When I did eventually bump into her she asked me what games I was planning for the prunes.

‘Got any suggestions?’ I asked. I have learned that the only predictable thing about Fizz is that what she

will say is always unpredictable. So when she suggested Strip Poker I was surprised and not-at-all surprised in equal quantities.

'Somehow I don't think it's a good idea.'

'Well, that's my only suggestion so now it's your turn,' insisted Fizz.

'OK. We have races.'

'What kind of races? Egg and spoon? How about hurdles? We could line up their Zimmer frames and they could leap over them.'

'Yes, that could work,' I said. 'But remember they are beyond ancient, so it might be better if we lay the Zimmer frames on their sides and they only have to step over them. The problem is that most of the Zimmer frames are being used as props for the tunnel. Mrs Kowalski told me.'

'That's right,' a voice whispered behind us and we both jumped a mile high.

'My stealth slippers,' whispered Mrs Kowalski with a triumphant smile. 'I think I shall have to get them patented. Now, Josh, did you get the spade?'

'He didn't, I did,' boasted Fizz.

'And I put it in your wardrobe while you were in the lounge watching telly,' I added, not to be outdone. Mrs Kowalski winked.

'You two lovebirds – it's so sweet.'

'She's not my girlfriend, Mrs Kowalski.'

'No? I thought Madame Dupont said . . .'

I could see Fizz anxiously shaking her head. Hardly surprising really. So was I. Fizz, my girlfriend? What was the world coming to? I thought I'd better try and change the subject.

'Fizz and I are arranging some games. We haven't told the Commandant, of course, because he'll only say we can't. We thought you might be a bit bored. Can you tell the others that if they want to join in, meet us up here at two o'clock?'

'What a good idea – that's when we're supposed to be having an afternoon nap. How clever. To tell you the truth, I have always suspected it's when Matron and Major have an afternoon nap – it's not for us at all.' Mrs Kowalski chuckled. 'Even so, I don't suppose everyone will want to come, but I'll see who I can get. Is it a secret?'

'Definitely.'

'Good. What are we going to play?'

'That's a secret too.'

'He means he doesn't know,' Fizz put in, helpfully.

'What I mean,' I corrected, 'is that I have some organizing to do.'

Mrs Kowalski nodded. 'I can't wait. The last time I played secret games was with my girlfriends on an airbase in Wales. I was given a dare and I had to put a worm in the Squadron Leader's tea. And I did. He was such a stupid man. He wouldn't let us do anything. We'd been trained to repair aircraft but he wouldn't

let us. He thought that because we were women we had no idea. We twiddled our thumbs and he'd give us jobs to do like practising sweeping the runway clear of snow – in August.'

'August?' I exploded.

'Yes. There was no snow, of course, and we didn't have any brooms either, so the six of us walked up and down miming the whole thing. Quite ridiculous. He was such a pompous ass.'

'I'd have put a snake in his tea,' grunted Fizz, and Mrs Kowalski smiled.

'We were hopping mad at the time, but it wasn't long before we saw the funny side. I've always been up for a bit of fun. And I got my own back eventually. I'll catch up with you this afternoon.'

And she slipped away, silent as the grave, which I guess is an unfortunate expression to associate with the oldest resident of Marigolds, but that's what came to mind, watching her shuffle off in her stealth slippers – unusual woman. I admired her. I'd always thought old people did nothing much except play bowls and then die, but here she was, flying Spitfires and digging her way out of Marigolds.

'What are you going to organize then, Mr Full-of-Bright-Ideas?' asked Fizz.

'Wheelchair races along that corridor upstairs.'

Fizz stared at me in astonishment. She obviously thought I was joking. I wasn't, and when she realized I

meant it she went from looking astonished to being delighted.

By two o'clock we had managed to locate three wheelchairs and get them upstairs without the management noticing. As it turned out, three was the right number because the only competitors to turn up were Mrs Kowalski, Madame Dupont and Miss Dash. Apart from that, there was only room for three wheelchairs abreast of each other anyway.

The ladies eyed the wheelchairs and looked at us expectantly. When Fizz announced a race to the end of the corridor their faces lit up.

'I have always wanted to do this,' sighed Miss Dash.

'*Magnifique*,' exclaimed Madame Dupont, before leaning towards Fizz. 'Him?' she said just loud enough for me to hear. Fizz made a sharp 'shush' noise. Heaven knows what that was about.

'I couldn't find any crash helmets,' said Fizz, 'but I did get some racing goggles from the physiotherapy pool. Just the thing, especially if you crash into a bath.'

Mrs Kowalski pulled on her goggles, tucked her hair behind her ears and gave the track a serious study. 'It's a shame there aren't any bends, or a chicane. I met Donald Campbell, you know.'

Miss Dash fixed Mrs Kowalski with her good eye. 'You knew the world land-speed record-breaker?'

'I met him at a party. He had very glittery eyes, I remember, a bit like you, Miss Dash, only two of them.'

Miss Dash snorted happily. 'You have a wicked sense of humour.'

'Oh, it's not just my sense of humour. I'm wicked through and through. Shall we race? Now then, you two mustn't cheat. I'm the only one allowed to cheat.'

'If anyone cheats it's going to be me,' declared Miss Dash.

'*Liberté, Égalité, Fraternité!*' chanted Madame Dupont, climbing into her wheelchair.

'*Jambon,*' retorted Miss Dash, and we looked perplexed.

'I think she might mean *cochon,*' explained Mrs Kowalski.

Madame Dupont gave a Gallic shrug. '*Rosbif,*' she hit back.

They crouched over their wheels and I shouted: 'Three, two, one, GO!'

Puffing and panting, they heaved on their wheels and edged forward, slowly gathering speed. Down the corridor they went, faster and faster. They probably reached speeds nearing two miles an hour. When they got to the end all three shouted that they'd won, but Fizz and I were still at the starting point so we couldn't tell. We had to have a second race starting at the far end, back towards us. That worked a lot better except that Fizz and I both got run over.

'I think Madame Dupont won,' said Fizz.

'Nonsense. Those two should be handicapped because I've only got one eye and one proper leg,' declared Miss Dash.

'*Stupide*,' hissed Madame Dupont. 'That makes no difference. In fact, if you only have one leg it probably makes you more streamlined.'

Miss Dash picked up her walking stick and tried to poke Madame Dupont and I think there would probably have been a fight to the death if Mrs Kowalski hadn't intervened. 'I suggest we do it another way. Why don't we get Fizz and Josh to push us?'

'We can't push all three of you at once,' I pointed out.

'Of course not, but we can do it in heats. You can do those two first. I'll go to the finishing line and be the referee.'

When she got to the far end of the corridor Mrs Kowalski called back to us. 'Ready, steady, go!'

I learned something straightaway. Wheelchairs are heavy and old people are even heavier. I'd laughed when I saw how slow the old ladies were at accelerating under their own steam, but it was almost as bad for us.

'Josh and Miss Dash won that,' said Mrs Kowalski.

'He's bigger than me,' complained Fizz.

'Never mind. I shall be the referee this time,' said Madame Dupont. 'Go back to your starting positions.

Josh, you push Mrs Kowalski this time, and Fizz pushes Miss Dash. Three, two, one, go!'

I would have won, but Fizz nudged me into the wall right at the start, deliberately, and I never had time to recover.

'We are the champions!' cried Miss Dash.

'You pushed me,' I complained to Fizz.

'No, no, that was me,' said Miss Dash, popping her left eye and polishing it with her cardigan. 'It's so difficult to steer a straight line when you only have one good eye.'

'What is going on here?' roared Major Trubshaw.

'Oh dear,' sighed Miss Dash.

'*Ooh là là*,' went Madame Dupont, as he came thundering towards us like a rogue elephant. His ears *are* pretty large.

We were all in trouble. The Major spoke to the lot of us as if we were kids. Mrs Kowalski was brilliant.

'How dare you speak to me like that! I am eighty-six years old, almost old enough to be your grandmother. If I were a few years younger I'd spank your bottom and make you stand in the corner.'

The Major ignored her of course and carried on blasting us, but Miss Dash kept interrupting with raspberry noises. Then I realized she wasn't pretending.

'I'm awfully sorry,' she said. 'It always happens about this time of day.'

'*Mais oui*, there was a Frenchman who made money

like that,' said Madame Dupont. 'His name was Le Pétomane. He used to play tunes by fixing a kind of trumpet to his *derrière* and he'd blow out candles too.'

'Madame Dupont!' roared the Major.

'He was very popular, Major,' she said. 'We all have to earn a living.'

But the Major was dead set on blowing us all up and he packed us off to our own little dark corners. It was back to the washing-up. I guess we were lucky he didn't spank us. What the Major couldn't do was wipe the smile off our faces, so it was well worth the row.

Funny way to earn a living, though. I'm definitely going for the astronaut option.

Why did Josh take me to his dad's? His mum's house can't be *that* noisy. And he never said what kind of noise because we kind of got talking about poetry instead. When he told me what his mum did I thought it'd be, like, you know, soppy stuff about angels and that, and how sunshine's a gift, but she writes about stick insects. How cool is that? I don't suppose anyone in the world has written a poem about stick insects before. I like writing too but I'm not an insecty sort of poet. I do more sort of parents-get-off-my-case kind of poems. You know, reality stuff. They're usually quite short. I did one about Lauren. This is how it goes.

Lauren – I hate you.

It might need a bit more work but the main thrust is there. Anyhow, I'm wandering off the subject, as usual.

Maybe all will be revealed on Thursday, when we shall go to his place to do our project work. Meanwhile, it is now Wednesday and he's coming back here

this afternoon and I have a plan, a BIG plan. It makes me tingle all over. He is going to LOVE it. And me too, hopefully.

Dad almost didn't let me out of the house this morning.

'You're not going out like that, are you?' he asked.

'It's what I wore yesterday.' This was not entirely true, but the effect was the same. It was just another miniskirt. What else am I supposed to wear? I've got great legs, I know I have. My friends keep telling me, enviously, ha ha. And I haven't got anything else to boast about, have I? My boobs require a magnifying glass and my mouth's a scrap-metal yard. I glanced down at my skirt. 'What's wrong with it?'

'Fizz, I know that teenage girls have to go through various mating rituals and that is why they wear such outlandish costumes . . .'

'No way is this outlandish!'

'. . . rather like female baboons sporting multi-coloured bottoms when they want a mate.'

'Darling, I don't think we need to know about female baboons at breakfast,' said Mum.

'I AM NOT A BABOON!'

'I've no idea why either of you find it upsetting. It's a scientific fact. That is what female baboons do and they pay no attention to whether or not it's breakfast time. What I was going to say, if you will give me the opportunity . . .'

'Do get on with it, darling,' sighed Mum.

'. . . is simply that a skirt that barely covers what it's meant to cover is hardly suitable attire for working in an old people's home, is it?'

I stared at him. Shocked. What was wrong with him? Was he turning into Matron?

'Father,' I began, formally, so he knew he was in trouble, 'I am sure you realize, because it's a scientific fact, that all old people are almost completely blind and deaf and I could turn up there naked and they wouldn't notice. So what's wrong with this skirt?'

'For one thing, you have to walk up the street to get there. Secondly, there are the people who work there. I don't suppose your boss up there thinks much of it.'

'You're just jealous of my legs, aren't you?'

Dad clutched his forehead. He appeared to be in great pain for several seconds. At last he let go, shook his head like he was trying to rid it of some midget goblin trying to climb in his ear, and said, yes, that was exactly it, he WAS jealous of my legs and to please go, go, go, and take the spade too, if I must.

'What spade?'

'The one you've got in your hand.'

'Oh, right, yes.'

I'll never understand him. So it was off to Marigolds, where I hid the spade behind a bush near the front door. Air-bags (I'm sure they're getting bigger) gave me the evil eye and kept her lips pressed so firmly

together you'd have thought they'd been stapled shut. (Good idea, Matron – go for it!) I waited for her to say something about my legs, skirt or baboons, but she didn't. Good for her. I almost told her she could have a smiley face sticker. But I didn't. Just occasionally I DO know when to stop. Anyway, I had some deception to practise.

'Was that Mrs Kowalski?' I said to Matron, and I looked concerned, which is not a look I do all that much so I had to act the part and be all actressy. I think I'm probably quite good at actressy-type things and I certainly fooled Air-bags.

'Where?'

'I thought I just saw her go round the corner.'

'Heavens above, don't tell me she's got outside!' And she went scooting off round the building. This was all part of my deception and by the time Matron came bustling back without Mrs Kowalski because Mrs Kowalski had never been there in the first place I had retrieved the spade, slipped it into the building and stuck it in the umbrella stand. It didn't look much like an umbrella handle sticking up but I had to hope that Matron wouldn't notice and she didn't because she was in a fluster by this time and desperate to get back inside, shut the door and keep all her prisoners locked up.

The morning was totally boring even if I did get a change of job, which meant I couldn't get back to the umbrella stand. I had to ask Josh if he could remove

the spade, which he did. He's so cool. He should be a spy, not an astronut. The only interesting thing about putting toilet rolls and soap in bathrooms is that I got to meet a few more of the residents – but still no sign of the mysterious Winkleberry.

Mrs Ogweyo asked me to get some food for Freddie. I looked round the room but the only living creature I could see (well, half-living) was Mrs Ogweyo herself. 'I must find him,' she said. 'We're not allowed pets, you know.'

'Has he gone out?' I asked.

'He's probably under the bed, but if I get down on my hands and knees I shall never be able to get up again.'

Aha – Freddie must be a pet, so that ruled out him being human, unless of course Mrs Ogweyo was even stranger than I thought. I looked beneath the bed. Nothing.

'I can't see him.'

'Are you sure? It's so dark under there, you might have missed him.'

So, Freddie was dark in colour. The possibilities were being narrowed down fast. Now I knew what Sherlock Holmes must have felt like. I could now infer that Freddie was some kind of dark-coloured animal, of a size that would fit beneath an old lady's bed. That meant it could be anything from a mouse to a crocodile.

'He's definitely not there,' I said.

'Oh, he'll be in the bathroom then. He likes the bathroom. He likes to jump in the bath and play with the plug.'

Right, that ruled out the mouse, but it could still be a crocodile. 'What sort of food does Freddie like?' I asked, cunningly setting a trap.

'Oh, the usual,' said Mrs Ogweyo.

I wanted to kill her.

'He does love those fishy nibble sticks.'

I gave her a commuted life sentence instead.

'I'll see what I can do,' I told her and she gave me a grateful smile. To tell the truth, I was actually feeling pretty stupid because I had only just twigged that Freddie almost certainly didn't exist. I'm sure he had once. Maybe before Mrs Ogweyo came to the home – sometime in her past, at any rate – she had once had a cat called Freddie. I think it was a cat. I had to accept that a crocodile was pretty unlikely. I was beginning to understand why Dad said conclusions were better than inferences. And I was beginning to understand Mrs Ogweyo too.

When I was four or five I had a pretend playmate. Her name was Lavinia. I thought it was a lovely name. It sounded rather fragrant, like 'lavender'. Now I know it's a stupid name because I once met a girl called Lavinia at a party and she had a long, long face with bulging eyes, like a cross between a giraffe and a frog,

and she managed to spill her cola down my front and tread on my foot by accident on purpose. I went off Lavinia after that, real and unreal. What were her parents thinking of, giving her that name? Lavinia. The way she looked I would have called her something completely different like Please Do Not Feed The Animal. But all that came later. Before that, I had this pretend playmate, because big sis, Lauren, (make protective sign) wouldn't play with me and I was lonely. Now Mrs Ogweyo had nobody to play with . . . except Freddie.

I saw Madame Dupont too. She asked me how things were going with Josh, and I found myself blushing. I did! And she saw! My head had suddenly filled with images of Josh and me rolling about on the floor.

'Ah, I think there has been something, yes?'

'Not really. We were just fooling about.'

'Fooling about is good,' nodded Madame Dupont, before waggling a finger at me. 'But don't tell me details. I don't need to know, as long as you are happy.'

'I gave him a neck massage but he didn't say much.'

'Oh, he liked it, but he's a man, and they don't know how to say what they like. They cannot express themselves, like women. They are strange creatures, men.'

Report for Wednesday by Josh Cameron and Felicity Foster-Thompson

Fizz thought the house would be empty and it was. Her father didn't normally get back until seven. Her mother worked late at the clinic on a Wednesday. Lauren was out. She was almost always out – her friends, her boyfriends, whoever.

'I don't think we'd better write about what happened this afternoon,' suggested Josh. 'It won't look good.'

'We don't have to say we got into trouble. We could say we arranged some games and the wrinklies enjoyed them. That would at least look good. You know, school would think, like, oh good, they're showing initiative.' She smiled at Josh. 'Hey, what do you think an initiative looks like?'

'What do you mean?' asked Josh, a trifle cagily. He never could work out where Fizz's brain was going.

'Like, we've been showing initiative. It sounds like you're showing knobbly knees or something. "Do

come and look at my lovely pair of initiatives, Vicar!" So what does your initiative look like?'

'You're mad.'

Fizz wished Josh would relax. She'd never get anywhere with him while he was like that. 'It was just a thought,' she muttered. 'OK. I'll do the first bit.'

Wednesday

Today was very exciting because Josh and I were allowed to swap jobs. This meant that, just for a change, I could put toilet rolls and soap in the bathrooms and Josh could make the tea and do the washing-up. When Matron told us that this would be the plan for today Josh and I were overwhelmed with excitement.

'I wasn't,' sniffed Josh.

'It's sarcasm,' Fizz pointed out. 'What's wrong with you this evening? Where's your sense of humour?'

'Where's your sense, full stop?' asked Josh. He sat nervously on the edge of Fizz's bed, among a farmyard of stuffed toys – dogs, horses, cats, ducks, teddies and several unrecognizable creatures. It reminded him of his own home, except that Fizz's soft toys didn't creep up on you unawares and surprise you in the shower, or leave their droppings in your shoes. Tomorrow he was going to have to take Fizz there. Josh gazed gloomily at the floor. Around his feet were strange,

bedraggled bits of knitwear that didn't resemble anything known to humankind, and cast-off clothing – a jumper, a bra, socks, trainers, a school shirt. His eyes rested on the bra and he wondered if Lauren would come home soon.

I could hardly contain myself as I told Josh that all these toilet rolls and bars of soap were preparing us for the world of work as adults. Josh said he couldn't contain himself either.

'No, I didn't.' He leaned forward and read the passage again. 'You're still being sarcastic, aren't you?'

'Well done!'

However, we have to report that Major Trubshaw and Matron are acting very suspiciously. The residents report all sorts of restrictions and this has led to Josh and myself suspecting that something fishy is going on. Residents are kept in their rooms most of the time. Some of them have said they would like to leave, but they can't. They feel as if they are being held prisoner, and certainly Matron behaves like a prison warder.

Fizz pushed back her chair. 'Do you want to do some now? I'm bored.'

'Not really.'

Fizz turned and looked at him. She bit her lip and

then went for it. 'You look even more tired than you were yesterday.'

'I think I pulled a muscle pushing that wheelchair. Or, more likely it was when someone pushed me into the wall at high speed, deliberately, because they're a cheat.'

'Oh, come on, it was a game. You're not still smarting over that? Tell you what, we'll get this finished and then I'll give you a massage, like yesterday. Will that make up for it?'

Josh flashed a dark look and said nothing, but *yes, that would make up for it*, he thought. Fizz's insides went 'Yes!' and she turned back to the computer.

In the afternoon Josh and I organized some activities for the residents. Not all the residents were able to take part, probably because they were confined to their rooms, but Mrs Kowalski, Madame Dupont and Miss Dash joined in. We all had great fun and they found the games . . .

'How do you spell "invigorating"?'

'No idea.'

. . . exciting. Miss Dash was the winner, even though her false eye almost fell out halfway down the corridor. Although the ladies liked the games Matron and Major Trubshaw didn't seem to agree and they soon asked us to stop. They felt it might be too exciting for the residents. However, that

is not what the residents told us. So now we are even more suspicious and perhaps the home ought to be put under investigation by the authorities.

Fizz did a quick word check. 'Two hundred and ninety-eight. One hundred and two short. My brain hurts.'

'Let me,' grunted Josh.

Mrs Kowalski is one of the most interesting residents. She has led an interesting life . . .

'That's two "interestings" in one line.'

'So?'

'Taylor says that's bad English.'

'Yes, well, as you may have noticed, Mrs Taylor is not here. Do you want me to do this or not?'

. . . During the Second World War she was a pilot, one of a handful of women pilots who delivered new aircraft to distant airfields. She flew Hurricanes and Spitfires.

'Is that true?' asked Fizz. 'Cool. Mrs Ogweyo is interesting too. She's got a pretend cat.'

'That's not interesting, it's just stupid.'

'I'm not so sure,' said Fizz thoughtfully. 'They're not allowed pets, and Mrs Ogweyo obviously loved her cat Freddie, so now she pretends he's still there with her. It's better than having no company at all.'

'But he's not there. She does have no company.'

'You may say so. Matron and the Major may say so. But what Mrs Ogweyo says is that Freddie is living in her room with her, and it makes her happy. It's her way of surviving life in a prison camp. I don't see much wrong with that.'

'All right, all right,' muttered Josh, who was getting desperate for material to write about.

Mrs Ogweyo is also interesting because she has got a cat called Freddie that nobody else can see because it doesn't actually exist. Mrs Ogweyo suffers from D.P.O. Syndrome (Delusional Pet Ownership). However, since the cat doesn't exist it is not doing any harm.

Tomorrow is Thursday and we look forward to discovering what our work will be.

'Now who's being sarky?' Fizz said brightly.

'That's three hundred and ninety-nine. Do you think Mrs Taylor will check?'

'I doubt it. Come on, I'll sort out that neck of yours. We'll do it downstairs.'

'Why?'

'Because Mum's private treatment room is down there.'

'Won't she mind?'

'Duh! She's not here, is she?'

Downstairs, Fizz showed Josh into her mother's

consulting room. Unlike Fizz's bedroom, it was clean and clear of clutter. In the centre was a low bed, with a small hole in the middle at one end. Josh eyed it nervously.

'Take off your shoes and shirt and lie face down,' said Fizz. 'Put your face where the hole is so that you can breathe.'

'I'm not taking off my shirt.'

Fizz folded her arms. 'Do you go swimming with your shirt on? Do you go on the beach with your shirt on? All I'm going to do is massage your neck and shoulders. If you want me to do it properly I shall need to use oil. Of course, I can always rub oil over your shirt if you prefer. I'll be back in a mo.'

She disappeared. Josh slowly removed his shirt and shoes and lay face down on the bed. It felt odd, shoving his face in the hole. He wasn't sure where to put his arms. Should he cross them above his head or have them by his sides? He was still fretting when Fizz returned. Josh's jaw dropped. She was wearing one of her mother's white uniforms. Fizz stood there grinning. She held her arms out to either side and gave a twirl.

'Do I look the part?'

'I guess.'

'Good. OK, lie flat, arms by your sides, and relax.'

Fizz tipped some oil on to her palm and rubbed her hands together. She got to work, kneading carefully and steadily at Josh's muscles. His back seemed so long and strong, and there was an archipelago of freckles across his shoulder blades. Fizz had freckles too, and she'd never liked them, until now.

'How's that?'

There was no answer. Maybe he was asleep. Fizz had got into the rhythm, running the heels of her hand up each side of his spine. Josh let out a long, low sigh. Fizz gazed down at her patient, heart in mouth. Surely he could feel the waves of love she was sending him?

There was a bright flash and Fizz spun towards the door. Another flash. Lauren stood there with a camera. She beamed at them both.

'Mum and Dad are going to love this!' she said.

I'm going to kill Lauren. I think I might strangle her with her bikini top. That'd serve her right. She waited until Josh had slid off home (very quietly, I might add, with his collar up, like a thief in the night) and when Mum and Dad got in she showed them the photos. And what did they do? They laughed.

'Oh, Fizz, darling, you look so cute,' sniggered Mum.

'Quite the thing,' added Dad. 'So what were you two up to? I see you've got Josh down to his trousers.'

'He's so weedy,' observed Lauren, peering between them. 'Don't you think he looks weedy? His chest is all puny.'

'He is NOT puny!' I shouted.

'He's fourteen, Lauren, what do you expect?' asked Mum. 'Don't be cruel.'

'Anyway, he doesn't fancy Fizz,' Lauren said tartly. 'He fancies me because he's a perv.'

'There's nothing wrong with liking older women, Lauren.' This was Dad's contribution and it put a scowl on Mum's face.

'Thank you, darling.'

'I don't mean you. It's a generalization. Some men go for older women. Besides, I don't suppose that Josh, being only fourteen, has any idea what kind of woman he goes for at all. Fizz, you may think you have successfully avoided my question so I shall repeat it – what were you two up to?'

'She was giving him a massage,' said Lauren.

'There's nothing wrong with that. Mum does it all the time,' I burst.

'To other women,' Lauren pointed out.

I couldn't think of an immediate answer to that. Mum studied me carefully. 'This is the boy you like, isn't it, Fizz?'

'Possibly.'

'And we come home and find him with his shirt off and you giving him a massage, all dressed up in one of my work uniforms. It is a bit suspicious, don't you think? What might have happened if Lauren hadn't come back when she did?'

That was easy to answer.

'I would have finished the massage – I was only doing his back and shoulders – he had a sports injury – and then he would have put his shirt on and I would have changed back and he would have gone home and nobody would have known anything about it and guess what?'

Everyone looked at me. I delivered the punchline. 'I wouldn't even have been pregnant.'

That stopped them for at least ten seconds.

'That's not the point,' Mum began.

'Isn't it? Isn't it? I think it is, you know, because that's what your grubby minds are thinking. For God's sake, I was attending an injured patient.'

Howls of hysterical laughter. OK, maybe I'd overdone it a little. However, it was all to my advantage because they never really recovered from that. They were too doubled-up to speak coherently. Dad managed to murmur something about his mind not being a bit grubby and Mum said it was sometimes but that was OK with her and I whizzed upstairs and locked myself in my bedroom. I rang Josh and told him what had happened.

'Lauren actually showed them?' he asked.

'Yes. That's how perfect she is, you see?' Silence. 'Are you still there?'

'Yes.'

'They laughed.'

'Laughed?'

'Yes. Ha ha ha, you know? They thought it was funny. I mean, they mocked us, Josh.'

'Not good,' he muttered.

'No, it isn't. Mockery is so cheap. And they said stuff too.' Another silence. 'Don't you want to know what they said?'

'I guess.'

'They thought we might have been going to, you know . . .' I couldn't help giggling.

'What?'

'Oh, you know. I mean, you did have your shirt off and you were just lying there and I suppose it might have looked a bit suspicious.'

'So what did you say? Did you explain?'

'Yes, of course I did. And I told them I wasn't pregnant so it's OK.'

There was a groan from the other end. 'Oh, that's great.'

'It doesn't sound as if you think it's great,' I said. 'It sounds like you're pulling the cross and fed-up face you've been making all day, the one you make when you think I'm stupid.'

'I don't.'

'You do.'

'I don't.'

'Yes, you do.'

'I'm not arguing with you, Fizz. I don't.'

'You are arguing with me.'

'No, I'm not.'

'See? That's contradiction, which is much the same as argument, so you are.'

He hung up. There's no talking to some people. I shall never understand boys. Or parents. Definitely not parents. I don't think they'll ever understand me either. I mean, on the one hand they want me to act like an adult, and on the other they try and stop me from doing the things adults do. Still, who cares? That was the best

ten minutes I've had for ages. Josh is so, so hunky. How could Lauren possibly call him weedy, not to mention puny? I could feel his muscles rippling under my hands. Mmm. How could Lauren say that? She must be blind. Or stupid. Or both. Unless . . . unless SHE SECRETLY FANCIES HIM HERSELF!!!!!!!!

I rang Evie and told her what had happened. That made her squeal.

'You gave Goat a massage! Oh my God! I can't believe it! Was he in the nuddy?'

'No, of course not. You're a sex maniac, you know that, don't you?'

'I only asked, Fizz. Anyhow, you're the one that bangs on about him being hunky-funky.'

'That's aesthetic appreciation, Evie, which has nothing to do with sex. I am simply admiring the human form.'

'The male human form.'

'Yes, well there's not much point in admiring the female human form, is there? I see that every day. Stop all this crud-talk because I have had a nightmare thought.'

'Not Mrs Taylor and her salsa tutor?'

'No, that's just horrible, nowhere near nightmare territory. I think Josh has got a secret admirer.'

'Never! Who?'

'Lauren.'

There was silence for a few moments at the other

end and then I heard a strange whiffling kind of noise. 'Hang on,' squeaked a tiny voice and there was a clunk as if the phone had been put down on a hard surface and the whiffling noise got louder until eventually I was pretty sure I knew what it was. Evie was laughing. She had both hands stuck over her mouth and she was trying to stifle a major snigger attack. I'd seen her do it many times at school, but I'd never been a long-distance witness, as I was now.

'Evie, pick up the phone. Evie? EVIE! PICK UP THE PHONE! DO YOU HEAR ME?'

'Hi, sorry, had to blow my nose.'

'You were laughing.'

'No, I wasn't.'

'Evie, you were.'

'Only a bit. It was funny. I mean, Lauren? Come on, Fizz, she's got the entire male senior school drooling over her. She could have the pick of any hunk in the school. Why on earth would she want to choose Goat?'

'Are you saying Josh isn't a hunk?'

'Well . . .'

'You are, aren't you?'

'Compared to the senior school, you have to admit he's kind of a small hunk.'

'Small? SMALL? What about Charlie then? If Josh is small, then Charlie is like a, like a teeny-tiny stringy beany thingy-thing.'

'Yeah, well Goat is . . .'

'G'night, Evie.'

I hung up. The trouble with Evie is that she's blinded by love.

Thursday:
Chameleon Heads
for Space

She dobbed us in. Lauren dobbed us in. How could she? We hadn't even done anything. At least I hadn't. All I'd done was lie there. And I can't believe Fizz told her parents she wasn't pregnant. She is beyond weird. That whole family is weird. Why did they think we were funny?

Still, cosmic massage. I hope she does it again, although I don't suppose I'll be allowed anywhere near her house after what Lauren did, which is a shame because it was nice there – not a single animal hair in sight – not a single *animal* in sight, which was even better. The only hairs I saw were long blonde ones on the back of an armchair. That would have been Lauren. Damn her eyes! How could she? Damn all of her, not just her eyes, everything, her mouth and . . . why does she have to be so beautiful? She doesn't deserve it.

Fizz is better than she is, and that's saying something. Strange creature. She's not as bad as she looks really. If she had a different head she'd be pretty hot.

Unfortunately she talks nonsense most of the time. I guess she's quite funny – on occasion – but she never knows when to shut up. Plus, she seems to think I'm some kind of Mr Grumpy, which I don't think I am. I know I complain sometimes but I only complain when there are things to complain about, which in my house is quite often, I admit. But that's not me, that's Mum.

Like yesterday, when I got back from Fizz's, Mum was in a panic because she'd lost Milligan.

'What is Milligan?' I asked, knowing full well it wasn't going to be human.

'A chameleon.'

'How big is he?' I wanted to know, running my eyes round the room.

'As long as my hand.'

'I thought chameleons were bigger than that?'

'Not the small ones,' Mum answered, with a weak smile.

'Ha ha.'

'Your great-grandmother used to keep tiny ones as pets. You know she was brought up in Africa? I remember her telling me she had one that used to sit on her finger. She'd point it at a fly and its eyes would swivel forward and a moment later the tongue would shoot out and hey presto! Fly gone.'

'Neat.'

'Their eyes swivel independently – very clever. It means one eye can look behind them while the other

is looking ahead, or above, or just somewhere else. Your great-gran did an experiment once to see if it would explode.'

'You're joking!'

'No. She was only eight or nine. A lot of her school friends had pet chameleons and everyone believed that if you put one on something red it would explode because chameleons can turn most colours, but not red.'

'Is that true?'

'Yes. So one day, when she was at home and nobody was about, she took one of her little chameleons because she wanted to know – she had to find out – and she went outside and she put it on a bright red poinsettia leaf.' Mum looked at me, eyes wide.

'And?'

'It didn't. It didn't explode. It turned a sort of muddy-brown colour. She was very relieved and a bit ashamed. She would have been mortified if it *had* exploded.'

I glanced round the room again. 'So we are looking for a small iguana-type creature that can camouflage itself? That should make finding it a lot easier.'

'Mmm. Sorry.'

We couldn't track it down. It was probably right under our noses all the time. Mum was worried about it wandering outside and I told her that if she left doors shut instead of wide open there was a better chance of

keeping it in one room. She ignored me, of course, and we didn't find it. I spent the rest of the evening working on *Escape IV*. It was almost ready. I only had to set the fins and wire up launch control. Space beckoned. As I worked on the fins I felt my fingers twitch. I was nervous, but of what? Was it the fast-approaching launch of *Escape IV* after months of work? Was it knowing I was involved up to my neck in the breakout from Marigolds? Or was it thinking about Fizz? Maybe it was all three. I was going into serious stress overload.

Marigolds was strange, jumpy. I bumped into the Major or Matron so often I wondered if they were stalking me. They are so creepy. The prunes were behaving oddly too. I had a strange encounter with Mrs Ogweyo, who told me Freddie was trapped on top of her wardrobe and could I get him down. For a brief moment I couldn't remember who Freddie was and had visions of some man lying curled up on top of Mrs Ogweyo's wardrobe.

'Freddie?'

'My cat.'

'I thought you weren't allowed pets?'

'Sssh. It's a secret. I keep him in my room. Nobody must know. It's a secret. He's up there. If you stand on this armchair you should be able to reach him.'

I pulled it across to the wardrobe. All this trouble for

an imaginary cat! The seat was soft but it just about took my weight. I could barely see over the top and had to grab the rim above the wardrobe door, cling on to that and hoist myself up a bit. That was when the soft seat gave way. My feet plunged through the elasticated straps supporting the cushion. I was so surprised that as I fell back I still clung to the wardrobe and pulled that with me. The end result was that I crashed to the floor with my lower legs still caught in the armchair, while the wardrobe toppled forward, pivoted over the back of the armchair and finally crashed down on top of me with such force that my bent knees, locked into position as they were by the armchair, splintered the door. I was pinned to the ground, mugged by a wardrobe. That must be a first.

'Oh dear,' sighed Mrs Ogweyo, sitting down on her bed and shaking her head.

The noise brought Matron in a jiffy. What a surprise. She'd probably been hiding round the corner, waiting to pounce.

'What's been going on?' she bellowed. I was silent and hoped Mrs Ogweyo would think of something. I couldn't mention secret Freddie. I wasn't going to dob her in. Matron lifted the end of the wardrobe with one hand, which was scary, and I struggled out from beneath the wreckage. I had half of Mrs Ogweyo's dresses wrapped around my legs. I looked across hopefully at the old lady.

Mrs Ogweyo's eyes bulged and she raised her hands in despair. 'What is the world coming to, Matron?' she asked, shaking her grey head. 'The boy said there was something on top of the wardrobe and the next thing – crash, bang – he's pulled it all down. Look at my dresses! I don't understand the youth of today. Is it a protest, do you think?'

I stayed silent. I knew it would be better that way. Just shut up and take whatever comes. Matron would have it in for me, no matter where the truth lay. First of all I had to clear out the smashed wardrobe. Then I had to move a new one from a vacant room into Mrs Ogweyo's room. Then I had to put all her clothes on hangers and hang them up. Finally Matron told me I was confined to washing-up duty for the rest of the day and she went steaming off.

As I went to the door Mrs Ogweyo called sadly after me. 'I think Freddie ran out when you made all that noise. He was so scared.' Yes. I knew it would all be my fault. That's the last time I try to help an old lady.

The only brcak camc in the afternoon when Mrs Kowalski surprised me at the sink, creeping up on me in her usual furtive manner. I asked her what she was doing down in the kitchen.

'I came to thank you for the spade. It's making things so much easier. We've made terrific progress. We should achieve breakthrough tomorrow.' Her eyes shone.

'That's fantastic!'

'Yes, and it's all thanks to you and Fizz. The Escape Committee can't tell you how grateful we are.'

'I'd love to see the tunnel – it must be amazing.'

'Tomorrow. It's too dangerous to take you there in broad daylight. Besides, one of us is down there at present. If you stand very still and listen you might just be able to hear them. The tunnel isn't all that far from where we're standing.' She put a hand on my arm and we stood, listening. 'Do you hear a faint scratching?'

'I'm not sure. I think so.'

'There!'

'Yes! I heard that. Is that coming from the tunnel?'

'Oh yes. Now then, tomorrow, I wonder if you can bring me a local map.'

'That shouldn't be a problem.'

'Excellent.' Mrs Kowalski let out a little breath. 'I don't suppose I shall sleep much tonight. I'm so excited, you see. Freedom tomorrow. I can almost smell the fresh air! Jack said there was nothing like the feeling of freedom after being shut away for such a long time.'

'I wanted to ask you, what was it like, flying Spitfires?'

'Not only Spitfires, but Hurricanes, Mosquitoes, all sorts. There were quite a few of us, you know. We'd collect the planes at the factory and deliver them to bases all over Britain. The Spits and the Hurricanes were the best: the engine throb, the power, the elegance

and, between you and me, Josh, they were rather sexy. It's true. It was dangerous too, and that's how I met Jack. I was flying a Hurricane when it developed a fault.'

'What happened?'

'Smoke in the cockpit – big danger signal, so I knew I had to land as soon as possible. We had no flight maps, in case they fell into enemy hands, so I hunted for somewhere, a field, a road, anything. Miracle of miracles, I saw an airbase. By this time there were flames outside from the engine and I could feel the heat on my legs. I was too low to eject. I made a very bouncy landing, at which point the cockpit burst into flames and the cover jammed. I thought, this is it, I'm dead. Bummer. There was a dreadful banging and shaking. The cover was smashed off and I was hauled out by a young American airman.'

'Jack?'

Mrs Kowalski beamed and nodded. 'He had no fire-fighting kit or anything. He simply reached in and plucked me out. We married a few months after the war ended. Now then, I mustn't keep you. If you don't see me tomorrow, you'll know where I am, or at least you'll know I've gone!'

'Good luck.'

'Thank you, Josh. You're a kind boy. I hope you and Fizz will be very happy together.'

I gulped and swallowed. 'What?' I croaked.

'I hope you and Fizz will –'

'Yes, I thought that's what you said, but what did you mean?'

Mrs Kowalski's eyes narrowed and she peered at me closely. 'You mean you don't know?' She sounded very surprised, though possibly not as surprised as I was. I shook my head. The old lady smiled and patted my arm. 'Josh, Fizz adores you.'

'No way!'

'Oh yes. And I think you like her?'

'Well . . .'

'Of course you do. She is quite lovely, and bright too.'

'Weird, you mean.'

'Thank goodness for weird, in that case. I wish you both good luck. Now I must get back to my little cell, which won't be a cell much longer.'

And off she went, leaving me with something to think about. Fizz liked me? *Adored* me?! Fizz? I considered the idea. She kept a scrapyard in her mouth, although to be fair, it would not be there for keeps. She wore glasses that made her look like some throwback to the seventies. I wondered what she'd look like with a different pair, or no glasses at all. Why didn't she wear contacts? Then there was the rest of her. And the rest of her was . . . when it came down to basics . . . a slightly smaller version of Lauren! She had the same rangy legs, the same curves and all the rest – just a

smaller model. Then there was her mouth, not the meshwork, but her lips that always seemed to be smiling and laughing. Oh yes, the massage! And that moment when I had her pinned to the floor. That was why I jumped off her so quickly. It wasn't because I didn't like her. It was because I was scared I *might*.

There was something else I hadn't admitted to myself as well. I was beginning to understand that annoying itch. It was there because I enjoyed her company. I looked forward to it without even realizing that that was what I was doing. She was sparky, funny, brave, and – what was that other word Mrs Kowalski used? – *bright*. Yes, well, even wise old birds make mistakes.

Maybe I should say something. Do something. On the other hand, suppose Mrs Kowalski had imagined it all? I'd look a right idiot then. I decided to keep a watchful eye on things. It was going to be an interesting evening. Fizz was coming back to my house to work on the project. That meant meeting my mother and the animals. I wonder how she'll cope. I wonder how *I'll* cope?

Hardly slept last night. I couldn't. I had Lauren on the brain. What had Dad said? Some men go for older women. Turn that round and what you get is . . . what you get is older women going for younger men. In a nutshell – Lauren and Josh! I could understand her fancying him. I mean, anyone would. Probably every female who'd ever seen him was after him. Chantelle Smith is, for a start. And Ann Burger, although she doesn't stand a chance because for one thing she's got a stupid name that sounds like something off the fast-food counter and for two things she's got a face like a bottom turned inside out and for three things she can't dance and just goes wavy like a bit of seaweed; really wet, stinky seaweed like you get at the bottom of the sea, which is where Ann should be.

Anyway – Lauren. Big sis. The sneaky moo-type animal. How could she steal Josh from me? My boyfriend! OK, I know *he* doesn't know he's my boyfriend but *I* know he is and that's the most important thing, isn't it? I bet that massage made him think.

I bet he's started thinking: *Wow, that Fizz girl, she's something else!* Yeah, and then he'll probably remember my teeth and my teeny-weeny boobs that I'm going to have to put in Gro-bags unless I get a lottery grant for a boob job – and instead he'll think – *Lauren.* Only it will be more like LAUREN in big neon flashing letters.

Star sign Slug was definitely in the ascendant. No wonder I didn't get much sleep.

At breakfast I passed a magazine cutting silently across the table to Mum.

'No,' she said, passing it back.

'What is it?' asked Miss Nosy, aka Miss Cow, Miss Boyfriend Burglar, i.e. Lauren. Her hand shot across the table and grabbed it just ahead of me. 'Want a Bigger Bust?' she read and she put on a sorrowful face and gazed at me. 'Oh, Felicity, you poor thing, have you got tiny boobies? Don't worry, big sis has got some binoculars upstairs if you want to try and see them properly.'

'Lauren, pack it in,' ordered Mum.

'Come on, Mum, it's a joke. I mean, what's she worried about? There's nothing wrong with her boobs. They're bigger than mine were when I was her age. Why does she have to make such a fuss about everything?'

'Perhaps she's copying her big sister,' muttered Dad.

'Thank you,' snapped Lauren. She pushed back her chair. 'I'm going to school. It's a place where educated people gather, people who know how to conduct civilized conversations without slagging each other off.' And she slammed the door.

Mum and Dad gazed at each other in amazement and then looked questioningly at me. They'll never understand. Never ever.

'She's right, you know,' I said and, holding my head high, I swept after her.

Because I had abandoned breakfast I arrived at Marigolds early, which completely threw Air-bags. (They are *definitely* getting bigger.) She was so surprised she forgot to say anything about my skirt. Instead she asked me if I'd caught the bus.

'What bus?' I mean, what's wrong with the woman? There isn't a bus. Matron looked at me for a few seconds, almost as if she was waiting for something. Whatever it was it never happened and eventually she shrugged and packed me off to work – toilet rolls and soap again.

The only interesting bit came when I was wandering the upstairs corridor and I heard a faint cry from somewhere. I walked quietly back, listening, but didn't hear a thing and I was about to go back downstairs when I heard it again. It sounded like 'Help!' in a squeaky voice. I stood near the stairs and waited.

There it was, and it *was* someone shouting for help in a squeaky voice. I hurried down the corridor and eventually traced it to one of the bathrooms.

'Help!'

I had to make a split-second decision. Should I send for Matron? Then I thought, no, whoever it was might die in the time it would take to do that, so I opened the door and hurried in.

Mr Winkleberry (as I discovered later) was in the bath. He looked up at me with a silly smile on his face. 'Thank goodness you've come, Miss,' he said. 'I've got my toe stuck up the tap.'

I grabbed a face flannel and handed it to him. 'I think you'd better cover yourself,' I said. 'Why didn't you pull the alarm cord?'

'It doesn't work.'

I gave the cord a tug and the buzzer went off. Mr Winkleberry appeared surprised.

'Oh, I thought it didn't work. It must be an intermittent fault. I do feel stupid,' he apologized. 'It's the fourth time this has happened. Why hasn't that nice nurse come? It's usually the nice nurse. I like her.'

'Nurse Evans? She's having a week off.'

'Oh, silly me, I forgot. Of course, she's gone to stay with her sister.' Mr Winkleberry was staring at me, which was a bit embarrassing. 'I haven't aged badly, have I? Will you marry me?'

'I'll see if Matron's coming,' I said by way of an

answer. Honestly! Mr Winkleberry must be all of eighty! I went to the door and peered out, which also gave me a good excuse to keep my back to him.

'Nurse Evans has gone to see her sister. She's got a week off,' chatted Mr Winkleberry.

'Yes, I know.'

'I like Nurse Evans. They're twins, you know, she and her sister, identical twins. Imagine that, two of them.'

'That's what happens with twins,' I said, feeling utterly stupid and helpless. I glanced at his foot. His left big toe appeared to be firmly wedged up the tap. I mean, how do you do that? I asked him.

'It just happened,' he explained, non-explanatorily. 'I think I'm prone to it. What do you think of that French lady?'

'Madame Dupont?'

'Yes. Do you think she'd go out with me if I asked?'

'I thought you just asked mc to marry you.'

'I could marry both of you,' said Mr Winkleberry slyly.

I never thought I would be so glad to see Matron come bustling through the doorway.

'He's got his toe stuck,' I said lamely and was about to add that I didn't think I should try and remove it in case it caused damage when Matron leaned across and just whipped his foot away from the tap.

'Oh, thank you!' beamed Mr Winkleberry.

Matron glared back at him. 'If you do that once more, Mr Winkleberry, I shall have to cut it off!'

'Ooh, Matron!'

'Pass me his gown, Felicity. Thank you. You can go now. I'll speak to you later.'

'But I –'

'Go!' snapped Matron, shooing me out of the room.

Boy, oh boy! This is such a loopy place! I decided to go and see 'that French lady' and warn her about Mr Winkleberry. Madame Dupont was rummaging through her chest of drawers. She seemed pleased to see me, which was nice. I have noticed, because I am actually a noticing kind of person, that people often seem to go quiet when I enter a room, or scowl, or leave the room altogether. But Madame's face lit up. She pulled a long scarf from the drawer. It was gorgeous – a deep blue colour with threads of gold and silver and ruby running through like glittery streams, and there were tiny sequins scattered here and there, constellations that flashed and vanished like the stars at night when clouds drift past.

'Can I touch it?' I asked, and she held it out. It was as light as a feather. 'It's so soft and beautiful,' I told her.

'My husband gave it to me many years ago in Venice and I've always treasured it. But, *hélas*, I have no use for it now. There's nobody to wear it for here.'

'That's a shame,' I agreed.

'I want you to have it. You wear it, Fizz.'

'But, I can't! I mean, it's . . . it's . . . ' I was speechless, which was probably a first. 'It's so precious,' I eventually managed to whisper.

'I'm glad you said that,' smiled Madame Dupont. 'Now I know for sure that you must have it. It is yours. It needs a young person, a beautiful girl, who knows how precious it is – she should wear it. It is yours. I give it to you now because it's your last day tomorrow and I may not see you.'

'The tunnel!'

'Oh yes, the tunnel,' nodded Madame Dupont and she began to chuckle. 'We shall all fly away like birds and escape this terrible prison we are in!'

It was lovely to see her so happy. I clutched the scarf to my chest. 'Thank you,' I said. 'Thank you.' I hugged her and kissed her cheek. She looked me up and down, then arranged the scarf around my neck and shoulders.

'*Mais oui, c'est très chic.* Now go to that young man of yours.'

'He's not quite my young man yet, but I'm working on it.'

'*Bien. Au revoir.*'

'*Au revoir!*' I laughed. And forgot to tell her about Mr Winkleberry. I dare say she'll cope.

*

A bit later Matron took me to one side. 'Felicity, I warned you to keep clear of Mr Winkleberry.'

'Yes, I know, but it was an emergency and I heard someone shouting for help and I had no idea who it was until I was in there and you never said why I should avoid him, I mean if you'd warned me I would have been prepared and it's a good thing I haven't been traumatized. In any case it was too late and I wanted to send for you first but I thought what if whoever it is is drowning in the bath or having a seizure on the loo, because I read once about a woman who went to the loo on an aeroplane and her bottom formed a seal with the rim of the pan and when she flushed the suction practically sucked her down the loo and she almost died and I thought what if you have suction toilets here and that could happen, or maybe the bath water was freezing and they were dying of hypothermia because you can you know, even in your own bathroom, especially old people and Mr Winkleberry was . . .'

'FELICITY! DO BE QUIET!'

I stopped. Air-bags was rocking back and forth on her feet as if she'd been mown down by a juggernaut. She took a deep breath.

'I wanted to say that I hope you were not shocked by him being . . . you know.' She reddened and I shook my head.

'Shocked? Oh no. I was on a nudist beach last year.'

Matron began to rock again. 'Really?' she croaked.

'Yes. Mum and Dad wanted to see what it was like.'

'Really?'

I nodded. 'Lauren wouldn't go, but I did. It was in France. They even had a shop where everyone went shopping, with no clothes on, not even the shop assistants. It was so funny.'

'Really?'

'Yes. Mum says she got poked by a baguette.'

Matron choked and went even redder. 'Really?'

'Mmm.' So then I asked her. It had to be done. 'Have you ever been on a nudist beach, Matron?'

I never knew Matron's voice could go so high. Normally her voice was quite deep but suddenly it went as high as a bird. 'No,' she squeaked. There was a short silence between us and then she coughed and restarted.

'I wanted to say I thought you managed Mr Winkleberry well. You should have sent for me before entering the bathroom, but you remained calm and practical in awkward circumstances. Mr Winkleberry is well known for doing such things. It's best to simply ignore him, as you did, and pretend everything is normal. We've had residents like him before, men and women. Sometimes they just seem to forget.' Matron sniffed. 'Evidently you are more sensible than your skirts. Well done. Get back to your work now.'

And off she went. 'Well done'?! Cosmic! So yes, it's been a good day I reckon, and it's going to get even better because Josh is taking me back to his place, his proper home. I think Mr Mystery Man is going to be revealed at last. Should I wear sunglasses?

Report for Thursday by Josh Cameron and Felicity Foster-Thompson

'No way do you live here,' said Fizz as Josh halted outside his house. At least Sheba had been reunited with his owner, so there was no manic Alsatian at the front. There didn't seem to be any goats at the window either, but Josh knew not to be misled. It probably meant they were asleep on the armchairs, or eating the television. Fizz stared at the front door as if she expected a tiger to leap out at her through the letter box. A small, thin tiger.

'But this is where Wacky-Woman lives,' Fizz protested, regardless of the pit she was digging for herself.

'That's right. Wacky-Woman is my mother and, according to you, a lezzie,' Josh reminded her. Blood drained from Fizz's face.

'I was exaggerating slightly,' she offered apologetically.

'Slightly?! She's my mother!'

'Oh God, I'm so sorry.'

'Why? Because I was born to a weird lezzie?' Josh spoke a trifle acidly.

Fizz wanted to die on the spot. How could she have been so stupid, so thoughtless, not to mention self-defeating? Josh would never forgive her. That was it. She'd blown it. She stared at the ground for a while and finally lifted her eyes to meet his. Josh was surprised to see them shimmer.

'I am so brainless,' muttered Fizz. 'I'm always doing this, putting my foot in it, saying stupid things to be funny and then they're not funny at all.'

Josh was slightly mollified and said she was only speaking what he knew lots of people thought. 'It's because Mum's on her own. There's only me, there's no man in her life. She hasn't time because what she really cares about is animals. The house is crawling with them and it drives me crazy, but the thing is, she cares. She does the things that others won't. She takes in animals and looks after them – whatever is necessary. She does it.'

Josh was surprised at how proud of his mother he felt at that moment. He started towards the door. 'You'd better come in if we're going to do that writing. Just don't be surprised if you get licked by a goat, or sat on by an elephant.'

'Elephant!'

'Joke,' muttered Josh, pushing open the door.

A tidal wave of animal odour crashed out of the house and slopped over Fizz: poo and sweat, dog biscuit and hay, wet fur and stale vegetables. Fizz gulped and stepped inside.

'Keep an eye on the floor,' Josh advised. 'If it moves don't tread on it. If it doesn't move don't tread in it.' He called out: 'Mum? Are you in?'

A distant voice drifted back. 'Garden.'

They went out to her.

'This is Fizz – Felicity,' Josh mumbled. 'We've got to write up what we did at work today.'

Josh's mother smiled and nodded and looked Fizz up and down. She rubbed her dirty hands against her sides. 'So you've found a girlfriend at last,' she said.

'No!' they chorused, quickly followed by a startled 'Oh!' from Fizz as she was nudged in the rear by a goat.

'Pack it in, Larkin. Shoo!' Josh's mum waved her hands at the goat and he moved away. 'Just ignore him, Fizz.'

'He reminds me of Mr Winkleberry,' laughed Fizz. 'But the goat's in better condition.'

'Someone at Marigolds,' Josh explained. 'He's a dirty old man who likes to pretend he's stuck in the bath so that the nurse has to rescue him. Unfortunately Fizz went in to help instead.'

Mrs Cameron looked at Fizz, a hand to her mouth.

'It was an eye-opening experience,' Fizz admitted. 'Matron said I did very well, which was pretty astonishing because she's like, well, like some dinosaur, you know?'

'Tyrannosaurus?' suggested Mrs Cameron.

'More like triceratops – you know, big, bulky, lumbering about. Matron is huge, isn't she, Josh? I mean, she's got a bust the size of Mount Everest – well, two Mount Everests I suppose.'

'I think I get the picture,' Mrs Cameron nodded. 'I guess you'd better get on with your work then. Be careful as you go upstairs. The last time I went that way there were two Polynesian Tree Snails trying to find a tree or possibly Polynesia itself. Oh, and keep a look out for Milligan. I still haven't seen him.'

'Chameleon,' Josh informed Fizz as they reached the stairs. Halfway up he let drop that chameleons exploded if you put them on something red.

'How do you know?' asked Fizz, a bit horror-struck.

'You don't want to know,' Josh said seriously. He was beginning to enjoy himself. Outside his bedroom he did a quick check to make sure that there wasn't a queue of creatures waiting to dash on to virgin territory and claim ownership, then opened the door and ushered Fizz inside.

'Wow!' she breathed, taking in the abrupt change of scenery. 'Do you have a cleaner or something?'

'I keep it like this.'

'Wow!' Fizz's gaze was drawn to *Escape IV* and she went straight over. 'What is it?'

'A rock-et,' Josh intoned slowly. 'And be careful, it's fragile.'

'Mmm. I got that. Tell me more. What's the story?'

'I built it. It's taken three months. It's what I do in my spare time. Not all the time, obviously, but, you know . . .'

'*Escape IV*,' Fizz read. 'What happened to the other three?'

'*Escape I* fell apart on the launch pad. *Escape II* barbecued itself by mistake and *Escape III* reached the record-breaking height of four metres before exploding.'

'Why do you call all of them *Escape*?'

'Look out there,' said Josh, beckoning her to the window. He waved a hand towards the back garden where his mother was trying to dig over a patch of ground while Larkin repeatedly butted her and two geese attempted to trip her up. In the far corner a donkey was peeing noisily on the rhubarb patch.

'I guess it does make sense,' Fizz said quietly. She was standing so close she could feel the heat from his body. She looked back at the room, at the walls covered in drawings. 'Are these the plans?'

'Yes.'

'Do you get them from magazines?'

'No. They're my plans.'

'You drew them? Are you sure? I mean, they're so . . . technical!'

'Technical plans usually are so . . . technical,' laughed Josh.

'Let me get this right,' said Fizz, going to *Escape IV*. 'This isn't a rocket kit you bought? It's your own design?'

'Yes, but I have to buy some components. I bought the fuselage for example, the engines, the electrics, but it's my design. This is the only *Escape IV* in the world.'

'Wow. Clever. When's the grand launch?'

'Any day now. Rocket's ready. It depends on the weather.'

'You're a dreamer really, aren't you?' said Fizz. 'I mean, like, you're always kind of organized, just like this room. It all seems so straightforward.' She glanced at the big red rocket. 'But this, this isn't straightforward at all.'

'It's a rocket,' repeated Josh.

'It's a dream,' Fizz told him. 'Your fourth dream.'

Josh shrugged. He couldn't look at her eyes. All at once they seemed too knowing, too close, so Fizz stood there admiring Josh's work and Josh stood admiring Fizz admire his work. Then he broke the silence and switched on his laptop. 'We'd better get this project done.'

Thursday

Today was a very busy day. I was asked by Mrs Ogweyo to help her get Freddie down from her wardrobe where he was hiding. (Freddie, as you already know, is Mrs Ogweyo's non-existent cat.) I had to stand on an armchair to reach the top of the wardrobe and my feet slipped. By mistake I pulled the wardrobe over on top of me. The door broke and the non-existent cat ran away. (That's what Mrs Ogweyo said.)

Matron came in and she was not very pleased. I am writing this down now because she might report the incident to the school but it was an accident caused by a non-existent cat. Matron made me drag a new wardrobe to Mrs Ogweyo's room, by myself, which is, I am sure, a breach of Health and Safety regulations, not to mention an invasion of my personal human liberty. (See our complaint in Monday's report.)

'That's good, I like that,' said Fizz. 'It sounds official. Did you hurt your back?'

'Only a bit.'

'I could give you a massage later.'

'I think maybe after what happened yesterday . . .'

'I didn't mind. They just laughed at me. Anyhow, you've got a nice back.' She began kneading his shoulders. There was a mirror to one side of where she was

standing and as she glanced at it her eye was caught by a small movement. *Escape IV* had just wobbled. She was sure of it. She continued pressing her thumbs into Josh's skin until she saw the rocket quiver again and a small, green, iguana-like creature appeared, clinging to the base of the red fuselage, just above the tail fins. Her whole body froze.

'Why have you –' Josh began. Fizz clapped a hand over his mouth, bent down and whispered, her breath hot on his ear.

'Don't move, don't speak,' she warned. Taking her hand away, she took a step toward *Escape IV*, and another. The creature took two steps further up the rocket, which trembled awkwardly on its stand.

By this time Josh had quietly swivelled round to see what Fizz was up to. The colour fell from his face as he saw months of work about to be destroyed. Everything he had worked towards, slaved over, puzzled out, everything was about to be wrecked by a LOUSY CHAMELEON!

And what on earth did Fizz think she was doing? She didn't know how to handle a chameleon. Josh reckoned it was more than likely she'd never even seen a chameleon. Probably couldn't even spell it. On the other hand he didn't dare move in case Milligan took fright. If the chameleon climbed any higher, or worse, leaped from the fuselage, that would be the end of *Escape IV*. At least his other

rockets had died honourably, but KNOCKED OVER BY A CHAMELEON was hardly going to be a glorious epitaph.

Fizz made a cautious approach. Milligan shifted a foot. The rocket shivered. Fizz drew nearer. Milligan shifted again and one eye rolled in Fizz's direction. The rocket wobbled. Fizz took three more silent steps. Milligan began to climb higher. The uneven weight distribution was reaching a crucial point. The rocket could topple at any moment and yet, despite the impending doom, both Josh and Fizz were fascinated to see Milligan slowly changing colour. He was trying to go red. Fizz's heart stopped. What if Milligan blew up!

She took another two steps. That did it. Milligan moved straight for the top. As he did so the rocket teetered and fell. At the very same moment Fizz leaped forward, clasped both hands round rocket and chameleon, then froze, holding her breath, wondering if the chameleon was going to explode in her hand. He was already a deep muddy-brown. He struggled against the pressure of her grip.

Josh raced from his chair and clasped his hands over hers. 'OK, slip your left hand out slowly until I've got Milligan . . . that's it, good, I've got the chameleon. Now put your hand on the rocket just beneath Milligan so I can pull him away and leave you holding the rocket with both hands. Keep it absolutely steady.

That's it, easy, brilliant. Hold it there while I take Milligan to Mum. Back in a sec.'

Josh flew downstairs and out to the garden. He thrust the chameleon into his mother's astonished hands and raced back, climbing the stairs three at a time. He almost fell into the bedroom. Fizz was in exactly the same position, crouched over the rocket, holding it safe. He gently settled it upright. At last they stood back and let out sighs of relief.

'Phooey – thanks,' said Josh. 'You saved my life.'

'I hardly think your rocket is your life, although I dunno – maybe it is? Is it all right?'

'Can't see any damage. Panic over.'

'I thought Milligan was going to explode.'

Josh burst out laughing. It was relief as much as anything. 'That was just a story Mum told me. You saw what happened. They go muddy-brown.'

'You sneaky trickster!' Fizz tried to slosh him but he caught her wrist and pointed at the computer.

'Time to finish off. Put something about Mr Winkleberry.'

'I can't!'

'School should know,' said Josh. 'It shouldn't have happened. It might not have turned out as well as it did. You could have been in danger.'

Fizz felt a warm glow inside and went to the computer.

This afternoon I was introduced to the effectiveness of the alarm system in the bathrooms. All bathrooms in care homes are fitted with alarms in case a user finds themself in difficulty, such as falling over and drowning. This is a sensible precaution because having drowned residents would not be a good advertisement for the home concerned.

I was working upstairs when I heard a resident shout for help. I went into the bathroom that was the source of the noise. Mr Winkleberry had got into difficulty. He said he had pulled the alarm cord but it didn't work. At first I thought this was careless of the home, but when I pulled the cord it did work. In the meantime I gave Mr Winkleberry a modesty flannel . . .

'"Modesty flannel"!' sniggered Josh. 'That's priceless.'

. . . and Matron came at once and sorted out the problem. In fact, Matron informed me later, Mr Winkleberry had done it on purpose, and not for the first time. I had not realized that antique people could behave like this and while this particular incident did not disturb me too much because I have been on a French nudist beach and seen everything . . .

'Really?!' asked Josh, sounding rather like Matron.

'Don't worry, everything was in French,' giggled Fizz, and went on typing.

. . . I mention it because I am disappointed that adults, who are always telling us to behave like adults, then go and behave like this. What kind of example is that for impressionable young people? Fortunately I am not that impressionable.

Fizz sat back. 'Can't do any more,' she groaned. 'I'm knackered. Must be all that excitement.' She did a word check. 'Four hundred exactly. Brilliant. I'm going home. See you tomorrow – it's a big day – the great escape!'

Friday: Escape of the Prunes

I have spent fourteen years living with I don't know how many different species of animals; fourteen years with animals doing animal things. I have seen it all. Mating goats on my bed, sex-starved stick insects, bonking badgers, fertilizing frogs, even a pair of copulating chameleons (not Milligan, he's divorced, apparently). And every single one of them was naked! But humans, female of course, no sightings.

And then there's Fizz. Seen *everything*. She's been on a nudist beach.

I

feel

SO

inexperienced.

And that's not all. When she saved my rocket and I put my hands over hers she was so warm and I could smell her skin and it was peculiar because she's weird and I'm not supposed to like her. She's OK, but I mean, I've never *liked* her. But now, when I think about her, my brain goes fuzzy and can't think at all. And

what is even more disconcerting is that she seems to know more about me than I do. How is it that girls always make you feel as if you've got half a leg missing and you can't keep up and you're hopping round in circles?

I wonder where that beach is.

I checked the weather forecast and Sunday is going to be clear and calm – bit of a breeze for most of the day but should have dropped by evening so it should be fine for *Escape IV*. I've prepared the launch pad, tested the electronics and rocket controls and everything is on line. All I have to do now is get Friday safely out of the way. My last day at Marigolds and the Escape Committee's too. I hope they make it safely.

I can't believe it – one thing after another. Sometimes it felt like three or four things after another. Where shall I start? OK, Friday morning. I got to Marigolds as usual. I saw Mrs Kowalski once or twice, drifting past with an enigmatic smile on her face, but the goons were around and she didn't stop to talk, although she did wink at me when I slipped her the map she had requested. I wondered just when they would make the break for freedom. I guessed it might be after lunch, when the prison guards sneaked off for their siesta.

I saw Fizz too. Late again. What a surprise. No, actually the surprise was her hair. She'd dyed it black. It suited her.

'My hair *is* black anyway,' she said.

'So why did you dye it blonde?'

'Blondes have more fun, so they say, although I think that whoever "they" are must have very small areas of experience in their lives because I have been blonde for three months and nothing like "fun" has happened to me. So where's it all happening? I've had about as much fun as a potato.'

'Sorry? Potato?'

'Ever seen a potato having fun? Of course not. Their life is totally medieval. They have their skin flayed off them with potato peelers. Then they're boiled, or fried or roasted or baked, and then, on top of that, they get eaten. Eaten! Would you call that a fun life? No. Neither would I. Standing in front of you at this moment is a potato. An ex-blonde potato. So I have decided to forget about pretending to be blonde and just be me, which is black. Black is my natural hair colour.' She flicked both hands under her hair. 'Dahdah!'

'It suits you.'

'Really? Can I have that in writing? In blood, I mean – written in blood. That proves you mean it.'

'You are beyond weird,' I said.

Fizz nodded. 'Right. And who lives with six million animals, tidies his bedroom without being threatened with death and barricades himself inside it at night so he can construct rockets that don't go anywhere?'

'*Escape IV* is going to work,' I said through gritted teeth. I shall never understand women. I thought I'd just paid her a compliment, saying her hair suited her, and now she was going for my jugular.

'I was going to show you, but I'm not now,' she said cryptically.

'Show me what?'

'What I'm not showing you because I'm not going to.'

'OK.'

'Aren't you interested?'

'No.'

'Not in the least?'

'No.'

'OK, I'll show you then.'

See what I mean! Where is the logic in that? Fizz was struggling with something in her bag and eventually she pulled out a toy black-and-white cat – something she had presumably selected from the massive collection in her bedroom. She clutched it lovingly to her chest, like she was about two years old.

'What's that?' I asked.

'Durr! Freddie.'

'Freddie?'

'Mrs Ogweyo's cat, right? I thought I'd give it to her.'

'Fizz, Mrs Ogweyo is about three hundred and eighty. Why would she want a toy cat?'

'Because every day she pretends Freddie is still there. I am going to give her something that will actually be there. It won't leave her. It won't run away. It's hers until, well, until she dies.'

'Then it'll be homeless,' I pointed out. So she hit me with Freddie and went off to find Mrs Ogweyo.

The morning was such a drag. I was jumpy. I kept expecting to hear of the breakout, but nothing happened. At one point Matron got me cleaning loos. I had to squirt disinfectant round them. Disgusting! No wonder everyone wants to escape. It can't happen soon enough. She'd have me scrubbing the bowls with my toothbrush next. Anyhow, it was vile. I wore two pairs of rubber gloves on each hand in case I caught something horrible.

Lunchtime couldn't come soon enough, and I escaped down to the shops with Fizz.

'When do you think they'll make a break for it?' she asked.

'Siesta time, or maybe this evening as it gets dark. That's what I'd do. Although, Mrs Kowalski said Jack made his bid for freedom in broad daylight. He must have had some nerve.'

'Was he spotted?'

'He and his friend disguised themselves as women. Apparently they were pretty effective and looked quite dishy.'

'Yeah?'

'They got as far as the end of the road and a small group of soldiers stopped them and started to chat them up and when one of the soldiers attempted to kiss him Jack sloshed him one and an almighty fight broke out and of course the pair of them were discovered. They ended up in solitary. Later on Jack helped on another tunnel but the war ended before the tunnel was finished so it never got used.'

Fizz pulled a face. 'I don't think I could ever do anything like that, risk my life and so on. They might have been shot.'

'Mrs Kowalski says you don't know what you might be like in a war until it happens.'

'Yeah, but that's like saying you don't know what you'll do when you have a shower, but you do, cos you get in and get wet so you do know all along really, and in a war you'll probably get shot and killed so it won't matter what you thought you'd be like anyway. I'd stay in the shower. It's safer.'

'Fizz, do you ever stop and wonder if you're making any sense at all when you open your mouth? Your explanations are about as helpful as the rocket-building instructions I once got that were all in Russian. Completely useless.'

'A Russian would have understood them,' Fizz said. 'So they weren't useless. By the way,' she grinned, 'what are we actually talking about? I've forgotten. Hey, you haven't asked about Mrs Ogweyo and Freddie.'

'Tell me.'

'She loved the cat. I knew she would.'

'They're all mad,' I grunted.

'I know. Great, isn't it! Anyhow, listen, I'll see you back at Marigolds. I've got to nip home quickly to get my cossie – I'm going swimming this afternoon.'

I almost choked on my sandwich. 'You can't just bunk off and go swimming!'

'I'm going in the physiotherapy pool, yoghurt-brain. Nurse Evans usually goes in with a bunch of wrinklies while the visiting instructor tells them what to do. It's just to hand out the floats and equipment and be there if there's a problem. It's not swimming, but hey, it's a change from teapots and toilet rolls. Matron says she saw from my school info sheet that I've done life-saving. See you later!'

I watched her swing down the road towards home. Swimming. Some people have all the luck. She really did have nice legs. My mind went on holiday to a French beach.

I was pleased I had remembered my little cat. He's so cute. He's got an extra-long tail and that kind of knobbly covering with a tiny bean filling that makes him very cuddly. God, I sound like I'm seven! Come to think of it, that's probably what Josh thinks. He didn't seem impressed when I showed him, but I had this feeling that Mrs Ogweyo was going to like him. You can fold his arms and everything. Well, not his arms obviously, because cats don't have arms – I mean his front legs. You can cross his back legs too, and he sits there with crossed back legs and folded front legs, looking like a cat-buddha. I expect Josh was jealous because he hadn't thought of it, not that he's got a toy cat to give Mrs Ogweyo and he couldn't give her a real one because she's not allowed so that just leaves his rocket. Don't suppose Mrs Ogweyo wants a big red rocket. Yeah, he's jealous.

I decided I'd better not let Matron see the cat or she was bound to confiscate it or keep it for herself so I kept him in my bag and when I had a few minutes to spare I snuck up to Mrs Ogweyo's room.

'I hear you've got a new wardrobe,' I began.

Mrs Ogweyo shook her head sadly. 'That poor boy, Josh. I felt so sorry for him, but what could I do? I couldn't tell Matron he was looking for Freddie. Matron frightens me when she's cross and she'd be furious if she knew I was keeping Freddie in my room. All I could do was sit there and let him take the blame for everything. I hope his knees weren't hurt. The new wardrobe isn't as nice as the old one, either. The door sticks.'

'Is Freddie here?' I asked, feeling stupidly excited.

'I'm sure he was a moment ago and I don't think he's gone out.'

'Perhaps he's under your bed? I'll take a look.'

'Oh. All right.' She seemed surprised.

I pushed myself halfway beneath Mrs Ogweyo's bed and pulled the cat from my bag. Then I wriggled out, holding him. 'Yes, he's here. I thought so. Look.'

Mrs Ogweyo stared silently at the cat. I held him at arm's length, his long tail dangling down, slowly swinging to and fro. Mrs Ogweyo sat and stared.

'Freddie?' she hesitated and raised her eyes to mine. I nodded. I didn't dare speak. She held out her hands and I passed the cat over. 'He always had such soft fur,' she murmured, squeezing the beanbag body.

'I'd better get back to work,' I said, and headed for the door. She called after me.

'You're a clever young thing, that's for sure. Thank you, Rose.'

Rose? I almost stopped and went back. Then I thought, no, it doesn't matter. She's got the cat. That's the important thing. God knows who Rose is, or was. Knowing Mrs Ogweyo, it could be a rhinoceros. She was a bit confused, that's all. But not so confused that she didn't know a real cat from a beanbag cat – I was pretty sure of that.

I met Josh at lunchtime and we had the usual crazy argument where he thinks he's terribly sensible and knows everything and then gets cross when I disagree. He looks really handsome when he's being serious. His face becomes more powerful. He looks funny too. I wish he could see how funny he is. He needs to lighten up.

I don't think he was very pleased about me going swimming either. Not that it was swimming. All I had to do was stand in the pool and be there in case any of the wrinklies decided they wanted to try drowning as an alternative exercise to the splashing the instructress got them doing. There were only three of them but, honestly, I've seen goldfish do more exciting things. After a while I began to hope that someone would try drowning. At least it would have given me something to do. Instead of which I was just getting colder and colder. It was the most boring visit to a swimming pool I'd had, ever. Eventually the olds were allowed out so they could change and I had to spend the next ten minutes retrieving all the floats and bits and bobs

they'd been using for their exercises and stack them away properly. Pure slavery, of course. At last I was able to go and get changed myself. I'd barely got my knickers on when the fire alarm went off and panic broke out.

It's astonishing that I didn't have a heart attack. I was standing right beneath one of the alarm bells when it went off. Almost at once voices began to call out. Fortunately I had been so bored most of the week I had read the Fire Procedure notices at least ten times so I had a fair idea of what everyone should be doing – assemble in the garden, basically.

I thought I ought to check the rooms to make sure they were empty so I started at the furthest end. Miss Dash hurried past in her wheelchair, muttering something about hating all these exercises they had to do, so I guessed it was probably a practice drill, except that at school when they have practice drill they tell everyone first of all.

The corridor was filling up with slow-moving prunes. Mr Winkleberry offered to help several of the ladies by putting an arm round them but they usually beat him off and obviously didn't need helping at all. Fancy being a sex maniac at that age. How can he even consider it? I mean, I've seen better-looking tortoises than most of the residents at Marigolds.

I wandered along behind them, checking each room as I went, and feeling like a shepherd with a wayward flock of sheep. At the door I met Major Trubshaw and told him I'd checked upstairs.

'Good. Sensible lad,' he grunted. First time he's been nice to me. Wow. I was thrilled. (Sarcasm.) By this time I had realized that maybe all this was Mrs Kowalski's doing and there was no fire; it was simply a diversion so she could make her escape. Mrs Ogweyo passed me, clutching Freddie. I was surprised to see Madame Dupont too. I had assumed that they would be in the tunnel. Maybe this wasn't anything to do with the escape attempt and there was a *real* fire.

Everyone tottered out to the garden. The last to arrive were three ladies wearing an odd mixture of swimming costumes, skirts, cardigans, towels and goggles, but not necessarily all of them at once. They'd come from the physiotherapy pool. Matron did a head count. That's when the missing member revealed herself. Mrs Kowalski. My heart sank and I crossed my fingers behind my back. I hoped she'd already made it.

'She must be inside,' growled the Major. 'It would have to be her. I'll go and check.' He turned to me. 'I thought you checked her room?'

'I – I did. She wasn't there.'

Matron was looking back at the building. 'I can't see any sign of fire,' she murmured, and at the same time we caught the distant sound of approaching sirens. 'I hope the brigade aren't hurrying to a false alarm. They won't be very pleased.'

'I'm going back in for Mrs Kowalski,' the Major declared and walked quickly into the building. I looked round for Fizz but couldn't spot her. My heart began to beat faster. She must be here somewhere. I pushed past the little crowd of onlookers but there was no sign. Panic set in and I ran towards the building.

'You can't go in!' Matron shouted after me.

'Fizz is still inside,' I yelled and disappeared through the doorway. I headed straight for the physiotherapy pool, because I knew she'd been there and I had to start somewhere. I hurled myself through the double doors and looked round.

'Fizz? Fizz! Fizz!' I yelled and yelled but there was no answer. I was about to check the cubicles when out of the corner of my eye I caught sight of something, something floating at the edge of the pool. It was Fizz, face down, slowly sinking. I forgot all about not being able to swim properly, raced along the side and jumped in next to her, and was surprised to find the water only came up to my chest. I lifted her face from the water and turned her over. 'Fizz, Fizz!' She didn't move. Right, what to do? Where had all that First Aid stuff gone in my head? Why couldn't I remember?

Sunday:
Lift-Off!

Get her out first. Quickly. I got her to the side, jumped out and hauled her on to the edge. Lay her on her side, clear her mouth of any obstacle. Roll her on to her back, one hand under her neck; tip her head back so her air passage is clear; kiss of life. I bent over her. I did this five or six times and then she coughed and spluttered and I quickly turned her head to one side so she could spit up any water. She spluttered again and took a deep breath. OK, get her outside. She was still choking but I didn't dare spend any more time in the building in case there was a real fire. I dragged her on to my back and stumbled down the corridor. I felt her body go limp again and said over and over again: don't die, don't die, don't die. We made it to the front doors and down the steps. I laid her on the grass and went through the whole procedure again. Tip head back, apply mouth-to-mouth resuscitation.

It was on the third attempt that Fizz's body gave a little jolt and she took a deep, smooth breath, and another. And another. Her eyes fluttered open, registered me bending over her, then she lifted her arms, wrapped them round me – and kissed me back.

I surfaced from that to a chorus of hoots and cheers. Miss Dash had two fingers in her mouth and was whistling encouragement. All the prunes were lined up and were watching the drama. A moment later two fire engines and one ambulance screeched to a halt and men poured into the building. Cool!

My funky-hunky hero! I mean, Josh actually saved my life. I didn't even know he knew all that life-saving stuff. He never said. Maybe it's standard training for a would-be astronut. Anyway, he saved me. Me! He saved everything except my glasses. I think they might be at the bottom of the pool and they can stay there.

The fire alarm got the old biddies panicking a bit. Me too. I mean, we were all still getting changed. Why do fire alarms have to go off at such inconvenient times? Why couldn't it have waited quietly until we'd finished dressing and then gone off? But no, it was extremely rude and decided to catch us all by the unawares. I'd got underwear on and I slung a T-shirt over my top and raced out of the cubicle, pulling up my skirt as I went. Everyone else was already hurrying out. I was the last, delayed by all that float-fetching.

I ran after them, still trying to do up the zip on my skirt, which means I was doing two stupid things at once – running along a wet poolside while trying to do something fiddly. I stumbled, tripped over my own feet

and fell headlong into the pool, hitting my head on the side as I went in. I was temporarily stunned.

It can only have been a few moments before Josh came charging in and rescued me. Then he gave me the kiss of life. Twice! I don't remember the first much, but the second was brilliant.

I was still lying there in his arms with everyone cheering when the Major came out with Mrs Kowalski. It seemed she'd been missing and he'd gone back in to look for her. Meanwhile the fire brigade arrived and took over, even though, as things turned out, there was no fire.

It took a while for everything to come to light. Mrs Kowalski had set off the fire alarm as a diversion. Everybody left the building except for her. Plus me, of course, but that's because I was practising deep-sea diving with a drowning option in the pool. Mrs Kowalski went to the tunnel and that's where Major Trubshaw found her – not in the tunnel but at the entrance, and the entrance turned out to be the door to a storeroom, the one with all the toilet rolls and soap and stuff. You'd have thought it astonishing that Josh and I hadn't noticed that there was a tunnel entrance inside the very room we had spent so much time in. The reason we didn't see it was simply that it wasn't there. It didn't exist. It had never existed. It was Mrs Kowalski's Freddie.

'She's done it before,' the Major told us, when Josh

and I went back yesterday, which, I would like to point out, was a Saturday. Exactly – we turned up at work on a Saturday. How weird is that? Well, we had to find out what had really been going on. Hadn't had a chance before, what with being carted off to hospital in a real ambulance and everything. Josh came with me. He wouldn't leave my side. He was brilliant and he looks so handsome when he's wet through. Poor boy, he was shivering with cold.

We both ended up in the back of the ambulance wrapped in blankets. I said we should share our body heat and that way we'd get better more quickly and the ambulance chap said he didn't think that was true and I said it was a well-known fact that when Native Americans got trapped in the snowy mountains and were dying of cold they used to disembowel one of their horses and climb inside the dead body while it was still warm in order to conserve their own body heat and the ambulance man said he didn't think that would be necessary and besides it wasn't snowing. Anyhow, while he was saying all this I crept under Josh's blanket anyway and I can tell you I was right. It was much better sharing.

Where was I? Oh yes, Major Trubshaw said Mrs Kowalski had done this sort of thing before. 'This was her fourth non-existent tunnel. We know when she's in a tunnelling phase because the spoons start to disappear. I found her outside the storeroom door. She was

searching her handbag and saying she was sure she had a key. She doesn't, of course. It's always been pretty harmless before, but this time she set off the alarm. She really does believe she's been tunnelling.'

'I think that may have been our fault,' I owned up.

'How come?'

'She told us at the beginning of the week about the tunnel and we believed her and we brought her a spade and a map and . . .'

Major Trubshaw gawped at us and then started to choke. His cheeks bulged out. He coughed and spluttered until I was getting quite worried. His whole body convulsed and finally he bellowed with laughter. 'Priceless!' he shouted. 'Absolutely priceless. Yes, I can see that might have helped convince her.'

'Sorry,' muttered Josh.

'To tell you the truth,' said Major Trubshaw, 'I think that's rather fine – that you two would make such an effort to help. You may have gone about it in a strange way, but the residents have enjoyed your visit. I can't deny that.'

'We thought *all* the residents were going to escape. We thought they all knew about the tunnel,' Josh said.

'They did. As I said, it's happened before. They know it's all a fantasy in Mrs Kowalski's mind, and they quietly go along with it because it's easier that way and it keeps everyone, especially Mrs Kowalski,

happy. There's not much else wrong with her after all. Like many old people she remembers the past more clearly than the present. She had a very exciting time in her youth. She flew with the RAF for a start.'

'She really was with the Air Transport Auxiliary?' asked Josh.

'You know about that? Oh yes. Did she tell you about her husband, Jack, and how he got shot down and made an escape bid? It all happened. They were dangerous, exciting times for those who lived through them. All she has now is old age and a room in a care home. It's no wonder she prefers to spend most of her time reliving her past.' He paused and chuckled. 'It's funny, don't you think? There was Mrs Kowalski trying to escape and she was the only one left in the building! All the others were already outside. Apart from you, of course.'

There was still one thing I wanted to know.

'Did Madame Dupont work for the French Resistance?'

'Is that what Mrs Kowalski told you? No. Madame Dupont was married to a diplomat and travelled the world, which is exciting enough.'

So that explains that.

Josh held my hand at the hospital. He said I looked better without my glasses.

'Of course I do. They were made in seventeen hundred and something and hewn out of crud by

cross-eyed, blind and ugly elves, their minds set on revenge against a world full of beauty.'

'You are so weird.'

'It's true, and if I didn't have parents who were also made in seventeen hundred and something I'd be wearing contact lenses.'

'Weird but beautiful.'

'Say that again.'

'No, it'll go to your head.'

The hospital kept me in for a few hours in case I'd been concussed. They contacted my parents and they rushed to my bedside, like I was dying or something. I mean, they'd missed that bit by hours. They did all the usual parental concern stuff and asked how it happened and I said it was because my glasses were so heavy they were falling down my nose so I couldn't see where I was going and tripped over my own feet etc., etc., etc., and what I really *really* needed were CONTACT LENSES.

'I don't believe it's been scientifically established that contact lenses prevent drowning . . .' began Dad, but Mum told him not to be stupid and of course I could have contact lenses.

Result! I was so excited I hugged Josh and his face sort of went peach, strawberry, beetroot, in that order, which sounds like some totally bonkers salad but that's Josh for you, and Mum said, 'Don't we get a hug?' So I had to hug them too. Then the doctor said could he

have one, but I think he was joking. Or maybe he's going to turn into a Mr Winkleberry when he gets old.

So there we are. Josh and I have still got to write up our report for Friday. God knows what we're going to put. But we've got other things to do as well. Josh says it's going to be a good evening for launching *Escape IV*, so we're going up to the park later, after we've done the report.

'We'll have to wait until the stars come out before we launch the rocket,' I told Josh.

'Why?'

'So *Escape IV* can see where it's going.'

'You are so . . .'

I shut him up before he could tell me, yet again. I shan't say how I shut him up but he didn't seem to mind.

It was cosmic telling Evie what had happened. She kept squealing: 'He never!' and I kept squealing: 'He did!'

'What was it like?' she asked breathlessly.

'What, dying?'

'No, you baboonomoron, when you snogged?'

'Um, sloshy.'

'Sloshy?'

'Yes, sloshy. Isn't it like that when you snog Charlie?'

'No. It's like . . . being in heaven.'

'Evie, you've never been to heaven. They wouldn't let you in for a start.'

'They would. You're just envious because my snogs are heavenly and yours are only sloshy.'

'I like sloshy. Besides, you are forgetting an important detail in this full and frank discussion we are having, Evie.'

'Like what?'

'Like Josh did something Charlie never did. He saved my life. Twice. Nurr.'

It's great having Evie for a best friend. I don't know what I'd do without her . . .

Report for Friday by Josh Cameron and Felicity Foster-Thompson

'What arc we going to say?' asked Fizz. 'We can't possibly say it all in four hundred words. We'll need more like forty thousand.'

'Leave out some bits,' Josh suggested.

They were at Fizz's house, sitting in her bedroom among the accumulated junk.

'Where do these go?' asked Josh, making a collection of CDs.

'What are you doing?'

'Tidying. What's this?'

'A shawl.'

'Has something been eating it?' Josh queried.

'It's meant to be like that. It's a radical shawl.'

'I didn't know there was such a thing.'

Fizz snatched it from him. 'Excuse me. I made that. It took me hours. You may use highly technical drawings to build rockets but I use my imagination to knit

radical . . . radical knitted things. Now stop tidying and being so motherly.'

'I was only trying to help.'

'You know what I mean. Tell me what to write.'

'Try starting with "Friday".'

Friday

Today was our last day at Marigolds. In the morning I gave Mrs Ogweyo a toy black-and-white cat, which she liked. She calls it Freddie. She used to have a cat called Freddie and she misses him. Mrs Ogweyo is a bit mad but I like her. I have dyed my hair black. Josh said it looked nice. I like him too.

'You can't put that! What's that got to do with work experience?'

'I can't think of anything else to say and, besides, I feel like it. I want to tell everyone.' Fizz smiled at Josh. 'Anyhow, I'm fed up with doing reports. Shall I put something about the tunnel?'

'What is there to tell? It never existed and we haven't mentioned it so far. Leave it out.'

We went to the shops for lunch. Josh had a prawn mayonnaise sandwich and spilled some down his front. He is such a dirty beast.

'You made me choke,' accused Josh.

'Excuses, excuses.' Fizz carried on.

I had a tuna sandwich and didn't spill anything because I am a neat eater.

Fizz stopped for a moment. 'Do you think neat-eaters are related to ant-eaters?'

'Maybe. They're both meat-eaters,' said Josh.

'And they might eat feet, which would make them neat-feet-meat-eaters.'

'Get on with it,' growled Josh.

After that I went home to fetch my swimming costume because Matron had asked me to help out at the physiotherapy pool in the afternoon.

It was very boring and cold in the pool. All I did was fetch floats and watch three old ladies jiggling about in the water. Then the fire alarm went off and we had to get out of the building.

As I left the pool I fell over and banged my head and landed in the water. I would have drowned but I was saved by Josh, who is tall, dark and handsome and he does the kiss of life, which is what he did on me, twice, so I didn't die.

'You can't put "tall, dark and handsome", it's daft.'

'I don't think it's silly.'

Josh says I shouldn't say he's tall, dark and handsome, but he is, so I don't see why I shouldn't. I was taken to hospital and so was Josh. He wasn't injured, he was just wet. (I don't mean jelly-for-brain wet, I mean wetly wet from saving me.) All the residents had been rescued and it turned out that there wasn't a fire at all. It was a false alarm.

After that we all went home, had tea and went to bed.

The End.

'That is never four hundred words,' said Josh.

'I know, but I can't be bothered to do any more. I'll tell you what, the hospital gave a copy of the report sheet on me banging my head. We can add that and it should make up the difference.'

'Cool.'

'So, we're all done.'

Josh pulled her closer. 'It's been a weird week. I didn't think Marigolds would be like it was. Nobody was what I thought they were going to be.'

'What? Like the wrinklies?'

'Yes. Even when they were being weird it kind of made sense – Mrs Ogweyo, for example.'

'It wasn't only the wrinklies. The Major turned out all right too. He knew right from the start and was trying to keep it all under control. Hey, I was just getting comfortable. Where are you going?'

Josh fetched his school bag. 'I brought you a present.'

'Really?' Fizz's eyes lit up and she bit her lip. 'What is it?'

'Guess.'

'Something sparkly?'

'No.'

'Something smelly?'

'Don't think so.'

'Is it cuddly?'

'You'd better open it and see.' He passed her a small, plain box.

'Nice wrapping paper,' said Fizz.

'Wrapping paper wasn't an option,' Josh explained. 'Go on, open it.'

Fizz slowly lifted the lid. Her face crinkled and she grinned back at Josh. 'It's just what I've always wanted,' she murmured. 'A chameleon. Milligan.'

I'm a hero. I don't feel like one. But then I've no idea what heroes feel like. I couldn't believe that Fizz was OK and it was because of me. Mum's really proud of me. But none of it is anything like what I feel for Fizz. It's astonishing. I didn't know I had those sorts of feelings. Where did they come from? I've known Fizz for three years but never felt anything like this for her. That annoying itch has vanished.

I don't know why I thought Lauren was more beautiful. Maybe it was those wretched glasses. I'd never noticed what a lumpy chin Lauren has. And knobbly knees. Not like Fizz at all. I reckon Fizz could be a model if she wanted.

This evening Fizz came round for the launch. Mum got to the door before I was halfway down the stairs. She had a goose tucked under one arm.

'Fizz! What an exciting life you lead! Josh told me everything.'

'Everything?' Fizz threw me a panicky glance but I shook my head. I'd told Mum about the rescue but left

out the bit in the ambulance and the snog in the car when nobody was looking.

Mum's eyes widened. 'Hmm, evidently he left out some bits, but that's a mother's lot and judging by your radiant look I can guess the rest. You look lovely, and that scarf is gorgeous.'

'One of the old ladies gave it to me. I love it. I wanted to ask you something. I hope you don't mind.'

'You haven't asked yet. How can I?'

'It's just that, well, um, I've been writing poetry for a while and Josh told me it was something you did and I thought maybe we could talk about it some time?'

'That would be good, yes, let's do that. Here's Josh, loaded down. Big launch today, I gather. Good luck.'

Fizz and I took *Escape IV* up to the park.

'I didn't know you wrote poetry.'

'There's lots of things you don't know about me,' laughed Fizz.

'Such as?'

'That's for you to find out.'

'Sounds like fun. What kind of poems?'

'Depends on my mood.'

'Tell me one.'

'OK, but you mustn't laugh. It's called "My Sister" and it's a one-line haiku.'

'Is there such a thing?'

'Yes, because I wrote one, OK? This how it goes: *Lauren – I hate you.*'

That just about killed me. I don't mean I laughed. The opposite. I understood. I squeezed Fizz's hand and she asked me if I thought it was too short.

'No. It's exactly right.'

We reached the park and as we passed through the gates I warned Fizz that the rocket might not work. After all, none of the others had.

'It might all go wrong.'

'It might all go right,' she answered. 'Will it ever come back?'

'It's got a parachute. It should drift back down and land somewhere.'

'Then what do you do?'

'Go and fetch it. Maybe do it again.'

'Oh.'

Fizz sounded disappointed. I think I knew why, but it was hard for me to let go. We found a flat spot. The park was empty by now. It was beginning to get dark and all the dog-walkers and suchlike had gone home. We set up the launch pad and placed *Escape IV* on the base. I checked thc controls, set the fins, made sure everything was wired correctly and charged up.

'Ready,' I said nervously.

Fizz looked up at the sky. Glittering pinpricks of light were beginning to appear in the east. 'Wait until all the stars are out,' she whispered. We lay on the ground, staring up at the fast-darkening sky, watching more and more stars appear. We lay with our heads

side by side, my feet pointing north and hers south.

'It's so beautiful,' she murmured. 'There are just so many of them.'

'There's the Milky Way,' I told her. 'And that really bright star down there, that's part of Scorpio. Sagittarius is next to it, then Capricorn.'

'Where's The Slug?'

'The Slug?'

'I thought there was a constellation called The Slug,' she murmured.

'You're mad,' I said.

'It's OK to be mad,' she said, her voice turning soft. 'I want you to tell me about the stars every night.'

'There's lots to tell.'

'Good,' she giggled, hauling me to my feet. 'Come on. It's now or never for *Escape IV*.'

I did yet another check. I uncoiled the wires from the launch pad to my control box and we moved out of range. 'Are you ready?'

Fizz stepped behind me and put her arms round my waist. 'Ready,' she answered.

'You can do the countdown,' I told her and I felt her give a tiny curtsy behind me.

'I'm honoured, kind sir. Five, four, three, two, one, lift off!'

Escape IV took off like a rocket. Couldn't resist saying that! But it did. It didn't fall to bits. It didn't barbecue itself or explode. It did what it was supposed to do and

just went up, and up, and up, until we could no longer see it, just the vast expanse of heavenly darkness vibrating with a billion distant suns. Space in all its glory.

'How high will it reach?' asked Fizz.

'A kilometre, maybe more.'

'Cosmic!'

'Almost,' I murmured.

Then there were just stars and silence, Fizz and me. We held hands, staring up at the heavens. Eventually I let out a long breath. 'That's that, then. A successful launch.'

'Do we go and look for it now?'

I swallowed. 'No.'

'But don't you want to use it again? You spent so much time building it.'

'It worked. I've achieved what I set out to do. It was magic seeing it disappear into the stars like that. You were right, Fizz. I'm glad we waited until it was quite dark. I don't want to see my rocket grounded. I want to remember it speeding to the stars, up there for ever.'

'You are such a romantic.'

'No, I'm not.'

'You are. Will you make another one?'

'No. I'm done with rockets. I think I might build my own telescope next, a proper astronomical one.'

'I know why you want to do that,' said Fizz.

'Really?'

'You want to spy on me, don't you?'

I laughed. 'Of course.' She lifted her face to me and the moonlight turned her brace into a tiny constellation. What was happening to me?!

We walked back gazing at the sky, talking, talking, talking. I felt wonderful. I could almost feel *Escape IV* still up there, racing towards the stars. My future. Fizz reached for my hand as we walked.

'Do you think my boobs are small?'

'I haven't seen them,' I answered and she tugged on my hand, hard.

'No, I mean it. Do you think they're small?'

'Not if I use my new telescope. It's going to be pretty powerful.' She whacked me in the stomach with her bag.

'I said I mean it! Do you think my boobs are small?'

'Fizz, for heaven's sake!'

'Well answer me, then. I think they're minuscule to the point of inversion and I want Mum and Dad to let me have a boob job and they are being so prehistoric about it and they might listen to you because you saved my life and that means you are Mr Important and you can ask for anything you like and I thought you could go up to them and say listen here, Mr and Mrs Foster-Thompson, your daughter Felicity needs a bit of help with her boobs so I think you should just cough up or else I might not bother to save her life ever again so

tread carefully, unless of course you don't think they are too small. So what do you reckon? Do you think my boobs are too small?'

Note from the Author

I found two useful websites while writing this book.

I am ashamed to say that until a few months before I began writing this book in late 2005 I was quite ignorant of the extraordinary story of the ATA. This website tells all: **motherflieshurricanes.com/historyATA.htm**

Readers may also like to know that there is in fact a thirteenth sign of the Zodiac – Ophiacus, the Serpent Bearer. Try: Summer Stargazing, Astronomical Animals.

Here's the link: **gorp.away.com/gorp/eclectic/nightsky/star_summer2.htm**

Welcome
HEARTS
to the INCREDIBLE world of
STUFF (aka Simon)
STUFF
JEREMY STRONG
ACTION!
ADVENTURE!
HEARTS
KNICKERS
Juggling
GIRLFRIENDS,
STEPMOTHERS,
KNICKERS
AND
TOASTERS
can be tricky!
WHAT DO YOU DO
WHEN THERE'S JUST TOO MUCH STUFF
GOING ON ...? ESCAPE!

Ask Jeremy

What's your favourite book/film/song?

I have many favourite books but one of my best when I was a teenager was **MY FAMILY AND OTHER ANIMALS**, by Gerald Durrell. I always liked animal stories as a child and the combination of animal observation and him gazing at his strange family as they while away their time on a fabulous Mediterranean island was hugely engaging and funny.

When did you start writing?

I have long stories I wrote when I was six, but I didn't really get under way until my middle teens, when I started writing poetry. I'd come across the poems of Dylan Thomas and fell in love with his wordplay and the sheer music of his poems. I decided I would be the next Dylan Thomas. Obviously things didn't quite work out like that in the end, but it was the beginning!

Where do your ideas and inspirations come from?

If only I knew! It's a case of trying to be open and alive to experiences, events, sights, sounds, feelings and so on. I keep notebooks, of course, and write things down, but very few of my notes end up being turned into stories. I can't force ideas to pop into my head.

My three tips for becoming a successful author

1. Make sure your main characters are strongly portrayed and interesting. They will help you write the story. Don't have too many important characters because you will find it difficult to keep track of them throughout the story.

2. Always try to put in the unexpected. It could be a character detail, e.g. one of them has a glass eye, or is an expert at rabbit-skinning. It could be something that happens or a bit of great description. Such 'events' keep the reader hooked and wanting to read on.

3. Always read your work out loud to yourself. It's a really good way to get a feel for your work. You also notice where you've made mistakes, repeated yourself and where what you've written sounds boring. You can then rewrite so the story gets better. And remember that 'longer' usually means 'not so good'!

There's no point in writing twenty pages of boring rubbish if you can produce two pages of finely tooled, engaging story.

Of all the books you have written, which is your favourite?

I loved writing both **KRAZY KOW SAVES THE WORLD – WELL, ALMOST** and **STUFF**, my first book for teenagers. Both these made me laugh out loud while I was writing and I was pleased with the overall result in each case. I also love writing the stories about Nicholas and his daft family – **MY DAD**, **MY MUM**, **MY BROTHER** and so on.

If you couldn't be a writer what would you be?

Well, I'd be pretty fed up for a start, because writing was the one thing I knew I wanted to do from the age of nine onward. But if I DID have to do something else, I would love to be either an accomplished pianist or an artist of some sort. Music and art have played a big part in my whole life and I would love to be involved in them in some way.

What's the best thing about writing stories?

Oh dear – so many things to say here! Getting paid for making things up is pretty high on the list! It's also something you do on your own, inside your own head – nobody can interfere with that. The only boss you have is yourself. And you are creating something that nobody else has made before you. I also love making my readers laugh and want to read more and more.

Did you ever have nightmare teacher? (And who was your best ever?)

My nightmare at primary school was Mrs Chappell, long since dead. I knew her secret – she was not actually human. She was a Tyrnannosaurus rex in disguise. She taught me for two years when I was in Y5 and Y6, and we didn't like each other at all. My best ever was when I was in Y3 and Y4. Her name was Miss Cox, and she was the one who first encouraged me to write stories. She was brilliant. Sadly, she is long since dead too.

When you were a kid you used to play kiss-chase. Did you always do the chasing or did anyone ever chase you?!

I usually did the chasing, but when I got chased, I didn't bother to run very fast! Maybe I shouldn't admit to that! We didn't play kiss-chase at school – it was usually played during the holidays. If we had tried playing it at school we would have been in serious trouble. Mind you, I seemed to spend most of my time in trouble of one sort or another, so maybe it wouldn't have mattered that much.